"Wait righ   ri- ous smile. He got up and strolled over to the jukebox.

When the new song began, Elizabeth's heart beat a little faster. She recognized it immediately. It was Nat King Cole's "Unforgettable." Todd stood at the jukebox and faced her, his loving look sending her back to a time before she ever knew the meaning of heartbreak. Back when true love seemed totally within reach. Back when Todd mattered more to her than anything.

Todd walked back to the booth and slid into the seat next to her. Their legs grazed under the table. He turned toward her and touched her forehead with his.

"I love this song," Elizabeth began. "It reminds me of . . . a lot of things."

"Me too." Todd tilted Elizabeth's chin upward. His deep eyes held hers for what seemed a blissful eternity. "I've never forgotten you, Liz. I don't think I've ever stopped loving you."

Elizabeth gently raised a fingertip to his lips. "You don't need to say anything, Todd. I know."

SWEET VALLEY UNIVERSITY®

Elizabeth and Todd Forever

Written by
Laurie John

Created by
FRANCINE PASCAL

BANTAM BOOKS
NEW YORK · TORONTO · LONDON · SYDNEY · AUCKLAND

SWEET VALLEY UNIVERSITY:
ELIZABETH AND TODD FOREVER
A BANTAM BOOK : 0 553 505718

Originally published in USA by Bantam Books

First publication in Great Britain

PRINTING HISTORY
Bantam edition published 1997

The trademarks "Sweet Valley" and "Sweet Valley University"
are owned by Francine Pascal and are used under license by
Bantam Books and Transworld Publishers Ltd.

Conceived by Francine Pascal

Produced by Daniel Weiss Associates, Inc,
33 West 17th Street, New York, NY 10011

Bantam Books are published by Transworld Publishers Ltd,
61–63 Uxbridge Road, London W5 5SA,
in Australia by Transworld Publishers (Australia) Pty Ltd,
15–25 Helles Avenue, Moorebank, NSW 2170,
and in New Zealand by Transworld Publishers (NZ) Ltd,
3 William Pickering Drive, Albany, Auckland.

Printed and bound in Great Britain by
Cox & Wyman Ltd, Reading, Berkshire.

To Robert and Anne Bloom

Chapter One

His lips were so soft and warm against hers, so tender and gentle. So achingly familiar. Elizabeth Wakefield melted into Todd Wilkins's strong arms. She was trying to remember why she was here. . . . Oh, right—she was here to return Todd's lucky sweatband. Then she was supposed to find her ex-boyfriend, Tom Watts, and try to make up with him. But the world was spinning so fast, and all Elizabeth's thoughts and good intentions drifted out of her mind. Todd pulled back to gaze deeply into her eyes and then reached forward for another kiss. . . . Elizabeth's lips tingled in anticipation . . . and then . . .

Slam! Elizabeth crashed into something large and solid.

"Whoa!" came a familiar voice, snapping her sharply back from memories of last week to the present. Elizabeth blinked, and Todd Wilkins

1

came into focus. He stood directly in front of her in the chip-and-cereal aisle, an overturned grocery basket in his hands. Cans, jars, and boxes had spilled everywhere.

"Todd," Elizabeth gasped. "I'm *so* sorry. . . . I didn't see you. I guess I was spacing out," she continued breathlessly, a nervous smile on her face. Did her daydreams of kissing Todd last week suddenly conjure up the *real* Todd right there in front of her?

She glanced quickly around her, glad the Organic Palace, Sweet Valley's popular health food store, was nearly empty. Elizabeth had been going stir-crazy and decided that a run to the store would allow her to relax her mind and stretch her legs. But now Elizabeth felt exposed and vulnerable, as if her romantic memories were broadcast across her forehead. *Thank goodness Todd's not a mind reader,* she thought anxiously.

"That's OK, Liz. If I had to be body-checked by anyone, I'm glad it was you." He steadied her with a firm hand, catching hold of her elbow. Elizabeth realized she'd been reeling, more from shock than anything else. Todd squeezed her arm lightly before releasing her. "Hey, I never realized that contact sports could be so much fun," he teased.

"I really am sorry," Elizabeth repeated,

clearing her throat anxiously. "I honestly didn't mean to tackle you." She hadn't seen Todd since they'd kissed last week, and part of her wanted to run for the exit. Her stomach fluttered uncomfortably. Why did it suddenly seem as though she and Todd were strangers?

Todd bent down to pick up his groceries. "Wrong sport. We call it fouling in basketball."

"Oh, uh—of course," Elizabeth stammered. "My mistake."

"Just making a joke, Liz." Todd raised an eyebrow.

Elizabeth and Todd reached down for a spilled carton of energy bars at the exact same time. When their hands touched, Elizabeth jumped as if jolted by an electric charge. *Get a grip, girl,* she warned herself. *Todd's just a friend, remember? People kiss all the time—it's an innocent sign of affection. All you did was kiss . . . as friends.*

Elizabeth licked her lips nervously, her heart thudding at the recollection. Ever since she and Todd kissed last week, she hadn't been able to think of anything else. Even Tom.

The memory of her night with Todd comforted her. Todd had rescued Elizabeth from the Zeta frat party; things had gotten out of hand, and she had found herself in deep trouble. She had unknowingly drunk too much from a spiked punch bowl and had fallen into the hands of a guy who then tried to take advantage of her. Todd had not only saved the day, but he had also treated Elizabeth with nothing but respect and gentleness. And later that night they kissed . . . and it was incredible.

So why do I wish I was anywhere but here? Elizabeth thought nervously.

"Liz," Todd said, interrupting her thoughts. "Could you hand me that juice can? It's right near your foot."

"Uh—sure," she mumbled, carefully avoiding Todd's eyes as she handed him the can.

"That's everything," Todd announced, extending a hand to pull her up.

Looking into Todd's kind eyes and feeling the warm clasp of his fingers, Elizabeth suddenly felt foolish. Her tension eased away, and she finally relaxed. *Why am I making this into such a big deal? This is* Todd *we're talking about,* she reminded herself. *I've known him practically forever.*

Elizabeth peeked inside his basket. "Carb beverages, wheat germ, bee pollen . . ." She looked up at Todd, her sea-colored eyes sparkling. "What is all this? Some kind of strange and unusual punishment? Or is it self-imposed torture?"

Todd chuckled. "Self-imposed torture. I'm

4

trying to get in shape for practice tomorrow. The coach warned us we're in for a long, grueling session. We'll have to be in top condition. He expects us to go far this season."

Elizabeth nodded. Basketball had always been Todd's passion, but she remembered how Todd had nearly blown it when they first came to Sweet Valley University. Todd's success as a major jock and Big Man on Campus went straight to his head. All the attention and glamour turned the guy Elizabeth loved into a cocky and arrogant stranger.

But then Todd's luck ran out, Elizabeth recalled. Todd ended up being suspended unfairly and thrown off the basketball team. It was thanks to Elizabeth's investigation that he was exonerated.

Now he's back on track, Elizabeth thought, beaming at him with pride. "I know you guys can do it, especially with you leading the way. Everyone says you've been playing better than ever."

"Thanks, Liz. I needed that," Todd said, reaching for a bottle of hydrating juice. He turned back to her, curiosity glinting in his eyes. "Now, I know why *I'm* here, but why is the most beautiful girl in Sweet Valley wandering around a health food store on a Friday night? You're not even buying anything." He gestured to her empty hands.

5

Elizabeth shrugged. "I thought I might check out what they have. Certain vitamins and herbs are supposed to help you study. Besides, I had some spare time to kill," she lied. Thoughts of Todd had been making her restless, and she needed some fresh air.

After she and Todd kissed, they both agreed that as friends, they had to set limits. Getting physical just wasn't smart. Elizabeth was still emotionally raw from her breakup with Tom. And even though Todd and his girlfriend, Gin-Yung, had agreed to see other people while she was away doing her internship in London, Elizabeth knew Todd still had feelings for her. Besides, Elizabeth and Todd had come a long way since they split up; they'd healed their relationship as friends and didn't want to ruin everything a second time.

Todd tugged a silky, stray wisp of Elizabeth's hair gently. "Where's the ponytail, Liz? I'm used to seeing you with your hair pulled back." His eyes held hers for a long moment.

Elizabeth managed a flustered smile. "I've really been scattered lately. I'm lucky I'm not wearing my clothes backward and inside out." She glanced down at her sleeveless striped shirt and pleated chinos.

"You look great, as always," he said with sincerity.

"Thanks." Elizabeth started walking to the next aisle, hoping they'd move on to another subject.

"I know it's been hard for you these last few weeks, with Jessica's trial and everything. I bet you're relieved it's over." He reached for a giant bottle of megavitamins and tossed it into his basket.

"No kidding! That had to be one of the most grueling experiences I've ever been through with Jess. And there've been plenty, as you know." Elizabeth reached for a nearby abandoned cart and tossed in a bottle of vitamin E. Pushing the cart in front of her, she grabbed some apples and mangoes from the fruit section and dropped them in too.

Todd smiled. "Jess is a trouble magnet. I guess things haven't changed since the old days. It still amazes me that you're related, let alone identical twins."

Elizabeth knew only too well that even though she and Jessica looked exactly alike, they were as opposite as could be. Elizabeth was the studious, dependable, thoughtful one while Jessica was a wild, fun-loving free spirit. But Jessica's carefree nature did get her into some pretty tight spots. Elizabeth frowned as she grabbed a bag of organic celery and a jar of low-fat peanut butter. *Someday Jessica will drive me to a nervous breakdown,* she thought.

Todd pointed toward the juice bar, interrupting her reflections. "Hey, Elizabeth, why don't we try it?"

"Hmmm . . . what do they have?" Elizabeth asked.

"Let's see, today's special is the carrot-garlic-oat shake. Sounds pretty healthy. What do you think?"

Elizabeth rolled her eyes. "Carrot-garlic-oat shake? You're kidding, right? I think I'll stick with Perrier."

"Well, I feel daring. Hey, you never know. Those shakes could be really great."

As they settled onto the vinyl stools Todd set his basket on the floor next to Elizabeth's cart and gave their order to the man behind the counter.

Todd fiddled with the hand-lettered menus while they waited. "Wow, Liz, listen to some of this stuff—brown rice parfaits, gluten and seaweed purees—ugh, I don't even think I can read any more." He made a face and tucked the menu back into its folder.

"Shhh," Elizabeth warned with a significant glance at the person preparing their drinks. "He might hear you. For all we know, these creations are his pride and joy."

"Jeez, Elizabeth," Todd said with a quiet laugh. "No matter how disgusting the food sounds, even if . . . even if there were *Clorox and Liquid-Plumr* shakes on the menu, you'd make sure no one hurt the chef's feelings." Even though Todd's tone was light, his eyes were intense. "You haven't changed at all, Liz. Not since . . ." As he trailed off, his smile faded.

Not since you *changed, Todd,* Elizabeth thought. *You let me and a lot of other people down. Is that what you're remembering now?* Her aqua eyes were soft with compassion. "Look, we've all changed a little. That's what college is all about, right? We're *supposed* to grow and learn from our mistakes."

Todd sighed. "You're right. It's time to think of the future anyway. Speaking of which—now that all the drug charges against Jessica have been dropped, do you know what's going to happen to Celine?"

"Ugh, Celine! I hope they keep her in jail for a long, long time. If anyone deserves prison, *that* girl does."

Just then two huge glass tumblers were plunked down on the counter in front of her. One was full of ice and came with a bottle of Perrier. But the other was full of something impossibly thick and strangely rusty looking.

"I'll drink to that," Todd said, picking up his shake and making a mock toast. "Here's to Celine's future. Long may she rot behind

9

bars!" But as he lifted the glass to his lips, he winced.

Elizabeth giggled. "Is something the matter?"

"It smells funny." Todd took a tiny sip. "It tastes *terrible!*" Todd's face was so comically contorted that Elizabeth had to bury her face in her hands to keep from laughing.

"Here," Elizabeth choked out between giggles. "Have the rest of my water. Looks like you need it." *It feels good to laugh,* she realized. *Not much has been funny lately.*

"Thanks, Liz, you're a lifesaver," Todd said, gulping down half the glass in a single swallow. "Do you want anything else? Or maybe you want to give this a try," he said, picking up the shake.

"No thanks. I think I've had enough healthful living for tonight. Let's get going." Elizabeth still laughed softly as she reached for her money.

"Hold it, Liz. It was my bad idea. So that makes it my treat," he said, throwing a few bills on the counter.

Elizabeth retrieved her cart, glad she decided to come to the Organic Palace tonight. *Maybe it was fate,* she thought. All her anxieties about running into Todd had melted away. *We're both on the same page now—everything's back to normal. Good.*

Todd hurried to catch up with her. "So, uh, Liz," he began hesitantly. "How are things going with you and Tom? Have you been able to work things out?"

At the mention of Tom's name, Elizabeth froze. A lump in her throat made it impossible for her to answer. She stopped her cart and stepped sideways, blindly bumping into a snack display in the middle of the aisle. Pain burned through her veins.

Stop it, Liz, she told herself. *Don't you go and lose control again. Not here. Not now. Not in front of Todd.*

"I'm sorry, Todd, but I . . ." Elizabeth struggled for an excuse, but none came. "I can't . . . I have to go." Pushing her cart aside roughly, Elizabeth bolted for the exit.

"Elizabeth—wait!" she heard him call. But nothing could make her turn back.

Your world is falling apart at record speed, Elizabeth taunted herself as she dashed out the door. *Quit trying to run away from it. Tom Watts is out of your life—for good.*

Life doesn't get any better than this, Tom Watts thought happily. *I have it all.* Stretched out on plush carpeting, he sighed softly and kicked off his shoes. The silken sounds of Miles Davis wafted from the massive entertainment system covering one wall; a tray of chips, cookies, and sodas was just a stretch away. *It sure*

11

comes in handy, Tom thought. *An attack of the munchies could strike at any moment. Why should I have to get up to satisfy it?*

Before leaving for an evening business appointment, Mr. Conroy had asked his cook to leave out plenty of treats for Tom and the kids. "It's the least I can do," Mr. Conroy had said warmly. "After all, you're doing me a favor by coming to watch the kids. I didn't even call you until the last minute."

"George, you're doing *me* the favor," Tom had argued good-naturedly. "It's a chance for me to get closer to my brother and sister."

Tom smiled as he remembered what Mr. Conroy had said before he walked out the door: "I'm a lucky man."

I'm *the lucky one,* Tom told himself, quickly shoving back memories of the woman who introduced him to Mr. Conroy in the first place.

Who would've believed that I would find another father at this point in my life? And not just any father—but my biological father. An unexpected lump formed in Tom's throat as he thought of his *real* father—not Mr. Conroy, but the incredibly gentle, hardworking man who'd raised him and given him his name.

Tom couldn't think of Mr. Conroy as Dad yet; maybe he never would. Tom had tried calling Mr. Conroy "Dad" for a while, but it just didn't feel right. Dad was the guy who'd taught him to throw a football, to ride a bike; the one who'd always laughed at his knock-knock jokes. Dad was the man who'd scraped and scrounged to help pay for college.

But Dad had been killed, along with the rest of Tom's family, in a horrible car crash. They had been driving to SVU especially to see Tom play in the homecoming game. After their tragic death the loneliness had been crushing. The only family Tom ever knew was gone.

But now Mr. Conroy was his family. He was more of a buddy than a father figure, and that was fine with Tom. *The main thing is that I finally have a family again. Life's given me a second chance.*

"Tombo, are you gonna move or what?" Jake, Tom's eight-year-old half brother, interrupted his thoughts. He pointed to the Monopoly board impatiently.

"Relax, dude," Tom retorted with a big grin. He rolled the dice and moved his piece, the shoe, six spaces.

Jake crowed and leaped into the air. "Wow, you landed on Marvin Gardens—and I own it. *And* it has hotels on it. You gotta pay me!"

Ten-year-old Mary groaned loudly and

flopped onto her stomach, her long, wavy blond hair draping over her face. "Ugh, I hate it when he starts winning. What a pain."

Tom smiled at his half sister. "Hey, don't give up. You and I haven't lost the game yet."

Jake smirked. "You guys know it's hopeless. I'm the Monopoly king."

Mary rolled her eyes and took her turn.

Tom laughed, then cursed silently when he nearly knocked over his soda. He'd never forgive himself if he put a stain in Mr. Conroy's plush, expensive carpet.

Tom was still awestruck by Mr. Conroy's wealth and good taste. The Conroy condo was incredibly beautiful and comfortable. The whole place gleamed and smelled fresh; a maid came in twice a week. The windows looked out on amazing city views. *Someday* I'll *have a place like this,* Tom thought. *Then George and the kids could come stay with* me.

"Oh, Tom, did I tell you my recital is coming up?" Mary wondered, giving him a shy look from under her lashes. "Maybe you could come. My teacher said I could invite as many people as I want. I really hope you can go."

"Sure," Tom said absentmindedly. "I'd love to go. It gets pretty busy at WSVU, but I'll definitely try."

Mary ducked her head and twirled her hair

14

around one finger. "Dana says I'm ready to play Bartók. And someday I'm going to play like Jacqueline Du Pré. She was the best—"

Jake broke in excitedly. "Hey, if Tom's going to go to your dumb old concert, maybe Elizabeth will come too!"

The mention of Elizabeth's name cut through Tom like a buzz saw. "Don't interrupt your sister, Jake!" he barked. Every drop of happiness inside him seemed to drain away.

Jake shrank back, looking crushed. Mary's face was shocked and pale. A terrible silence came over them.

Look what you've done, Tom scolded himself. *Jake didn't mean to say anything wrong. What kind of an ogre are you?* He stiffened. "Jake, I'm sorry. I didn't mean to be a jerk," he said. "I was thinking of something else, and I got mad for a second." He reached his hand across the game board. "Friends?" He caught Jake's smoldering expression. "Or would you rather just punch me?"

Jake's scowl dissolved into a grin. He grabbed Tom's hand. "Maybe I'll hit you another time. If you give me one of your hotels, I'll forgive you."

Mary groaned loudly. "He is a little rat."

Tom laughed and handed over a hotel. "Nope. Jake's just a good businessman. A very good businessman."

Everything was fine now—on the outside. But on the inside, Tom was disgusted with himself. *Way to go, Watts. You chewed out an innocent kid just because you and Liz*— Tom flinched, feeling the sting that came from just thinking about her. Elizabeth had hurt him so badly, he doubted the scars would ever fade. *I thought Elizabeth and I were going to be together forever. We were a team—at work and in love. We shared the same dreams, the same values, the same everything. Or so I thought.*

Tom closed his eyes briefly. Elizabeth had been the woman who introduced George Conroy into Tom's life. Elizabeth had been helping Mr. Conroy track down his long-lost son, never knowing it was Tom.

And then she'd betrayed them both. Elizabeth had turned jealous and petty, accusing Tom's father of coming on to her. His own father! It was so underhanded that at first Tom couldn't believe Elizabeth was capable of such a thing. But she had stubbornly stuck to her guns. Just the thought of it turned Tom's stomach.

Well, Liz, you drove a stake through my heart, but I'm not going to let you ruin my life anymore. I've got my father; I've got my family. I don't need anyone else.

"I won, I won!" shrieked Jake, climbing

onto Tom's back and pulling his hair. "Yippee!" He leaped off Tom and did a mad dance around the coffee table. "I am the *win*-ner!"

Mary jumped up. "Well, I came in second. Guess that means you lost, Tom, but we still love you!" she sang, throwing her arms around Tom's neck.

The kids' exuberance was so infectious, Tom could feel his depression slipping away quickly. With a cartoonish growl Tom picked up Mary under her arms and spun her around.

"Whee!" Mary giggled. "Don't tickle me, Tom!"

Jake jumped up and down. "Me next! My turn!"

Tom put Mary down and spun around his little half brother, who kicked his legs with glee.

"Ugh! I'm dizzy!" Mary groaned as she rolled around on the den carpet. "You're fun, Tom. You're so crazy."

"I'm not crazy," Tom said, stopping to plunk Jake down on the couch. He crept up behind Mary. "I'm totally *insane!*" Mary squealed as Tom tickled her mercilessly.

Jake stood up on the arm of the sofa and pretended to be a surfer. "Hey, dude, you really know how to party."

Yeah, right, Tom thought. *I used to know how to party. They didn't call me Wildman Watts for nothing.* A smile crept across his face as he watched his siblings dance around the den. *A party. Yeah, that's what I need. Maybe it's time I stopped being Mr. Serious. Maybe it's time I dusted old Wildman off and let myself have some fun for a change.*

I'm going to faint, Jessica Wakefield thought dreamily. *But I don't care.* She and Nick Fox had been kissing passionately for so long, she was out of breath.

Nick's lips moved across to her cheek, lingering at the dimple on the left side of her mouth, and then returned to her waiting lips. This was bliss.

"This is terrible, Jess," he said softly, with a teasing gleam in his deep green eyes. "For some reason I have to keep kissing you . . . and kissing you." He scooped up her hand and traced each finger with his lips.

Nick and Jessica were curled together on a king-size blanket beside the ocean, the sand soft as whipped cream beneath them. The air was balmy and tangy, the liquid black sky lit with ice white stars.

"I think I need help," Nick murmured, pulling her closer and kissing her forehead. "Somebody stop me."

"You're out of luck," Jessica declared, snuggling against his shoulder. "There's no one

18

around to save you. I guess you'll just have to keep on kissing me."

Nick sat up, his white teeth gleaming against the rugged tan of his face. *He looks like a Greek statue in the moonlight,* Jessica thought.

Nick reached for the picnic basket to take out a soda. The basket tipped over, revealing half-eaten sandwiches and fruit. Jessica giggled. They had meant to have a stargazing picnic on the beach, but it had developed into a lip-locking fest too quickly for them to actually eat much.

"You know, we're *supposed* to be looking at the stars," Jessica jokingly reminded him, pulling the blanket around her feet.

"Oh, yeah," Nick agreed. "I forgot." He put the bottle aside and swept Jessica into his arms, gazing contentedly into her eyes before turning toward the sky.

Jessica sighed. She couldn't believe that only a short while ago she'd been sitting in jail, convinced she'd spend the rest of her young life there. And she'd been innocent—nosy, but totally innocent. Nick Fox had been so mysterious that Jessica had been convinced he was some kind of double agent. She'd listened in on one of his phone conversations, disabled his car, and set out to meet with the operative who she thought would hand her the papers that would prove Nick was a spy. But instead she'd been surrounded by cops, handcuffed, and dragged to the police station like a common criminal.

The biggest shock had been the truth about Nick. The man she had loved was the man who had put her in handcuffs! Nick had been working undercover, trying to expose a campus drug ring. And he had been convinced that Jessica was guilty until he discovered the real culprit, saving Jessica from a certain prison sentence at the very last second.

My hero, Jessica thought, sighing more loudly this time. *Unbelievably sexy and dangerous, but law-abiding too. How did I get so lucky?*

"Nick." She said his name out loud.

"What, Jess?" He was still examining the stars. "Look, there's the Crab Nebula—"

Jessica bolted upright, annoyed that Nick's attention had strayed from her. *How can he prefer astronomy to me at a moment like this?* she thought. "Are you listening to me?"

He gave her a hug. "Always. What's up, sunshine?"

Jessica smiled and relaxed against him. "I was just wondering if we're going to get together tomorrow night. After all, it *is* the weekend."

When Nick didn't answer, Jessica turned to

glare at him. "You *can't* be working," she said quickly, then thought again. *With Nick, you never know. The guy practically lives at the police station.*

Nick shook his head. "No, it's not that. I just promised the folks I'd come over for dinner. They've been after me about it for weeks." He smiled apologetically. "I love them and everything, but they just don't give up."

Jessica felt her brows draw together in a scowl. *I can't believe this,* she thought. *He didn't even ask me if I wanted to go. Why wouldn't he want to introduce me to his parents?*

She tossed back her hair, her eyes glittering indignantly. "I'm coming too, I hope. Saturday is one of the few days I ever get to see you. Besides, I'd like to meet your mom and dad."

Nick shook his head quickly. "Sorry, Jess, but I don't think so." He seemed to catch the stormy expression on her face. "Wait—before you attack me, let me explain. My parents . . . well, really, my *mother* is not the easiest person to get along with. I mean, she's great, and I love her, but she's, um, how shall I say . . . *difficult.*"

"But Nick, I'm *great* with difficult people. They're my specialty." She fluttered her long lashes at him. "I can handle people; ask anyone. There isn't a difficult person in this world that I couldn't charm. Honest."

Nick laughed. "I'm sure that's true, but the timing's just not right."

"I don't see why not," Jessica argued. "Tomorrow night is the perfect time for all of us to get to know one another."

"Look, Jess, I want to prepare my parents before they meet you—," Nick began.

"Prepare!" Jessica pulled herself from Nick's arms and leaped to her feet, her face reddening. "Just what do you mean?"

"My parents are a little overprotective—a little fussy," Nick said quickly. "My mother can be unpredictable—"

"Is this about my false arrest, Nick? Because you know I was totally innocent!"

Nick shook his head and opened his mouth to speak again, but Jessica didn't grant him the luxury.

"So what you're saying is I'm such a terrible, unworthy person that you have to *explain* me to your *fussy* parents! How dare you say that!"

"Calm down, Jess; that's not exactly what I meant."

Jessica stared down at him, her eyes practically shooting sparks. "Oh, not *exactly*, huh? Let me guess *exactly* what you're going to tell your parents about me—that I'm not good enough or sophisticated enough?" Jessica swept up her new mules, jammed her feet into them, and started rapidly across the beach. She stomped hard as she walked, sand flying out with every angry step.

"Jessica, you're jumping to conclusions," he called.

Jessica didn't even turn around. "Forget it. If I'm not good enough for your parents, Nick Fox, then I must not be good enough for you!"

Chapter
Two

"Elizabeth, please stop!" Todd broke into a run and immediately tripped over the wheel of Elizabeth's abandoned cart. He dropped his own basket and it skidded across the linoleum floor, knocking over a stack of newspapers. *What's gotten into her?* Todd thought anxiously. *She tore out of here like the place was on fire.*

"Hey, buddy—," the cashier yelled as Todd dashed toward the exit of the health food store.

Todd waved him off, intent on finding Elizabeth. He immediately spotted her golden hair gleaming under the parking lot lights. She was slumped over against her Jeep, shoulders shaking, her face buried in her hands. The sight made Todd's heart ache as he jogged over to her.

"What happened, Liz?" Todd asked. "Did I

say something wrong? I'm sorry about bringing up Tom, but—"

Elizabeth's tearful gaze stopped him cold. Shrugging helplessly, she turned away again.

"C'mon, you can talk to me," he coaxed. "We're friends, right? You can tell me anything. You know that."

"You're right." A shaky smile trembled on her lips. "But—but I really can't talk about it right now." She stared off into the distance.

"So you're not mad at me," Todd said hopefully. "Am I right?"

"I'm not mad at you, Todd," she replied with a hint of exasperation. "I just can't—"

"So . . . is it Tom?" Todd watched Elizabeth's delicate face closely, glad to see she didn't run away at the mention of his name.

Elizabeth crossed her arms indignantly and turned to him, her gaze turning to cold steel. "Of course not. That's all behind me now." She raised her chin. "I'm totally over it."

"Then what happened? Nobody runs off like that unless something's *really* wrong." Todd watched as Elizabeth blushed and lowered her eyes. *She's lying,* he thought. *Liz is still hung up on Tom and just won't admit it.*

"I'm just . . . I don't know . . . going through a confusing time in my life," Elizabeth answered in a low voice. "Look, Todd, right now I need calm in my life . . . and once that happens, I'll be fine."

She may say that now, Todd thought, *but her eyes tell me it's not going to happen anytime soon.*

Suddenly music flooded the nearly deserted parking lot. The mall's loudspeakers poured out an easy-listening version of "Yesterday," the Beatles classic. It sounded sappy, but as Todd sang the lyrics silently in his head, their meaning hit home. Without realizing it, he reached out for Elizabeth's hand.

Elizabeth hesitated only a second before she slipped her slender hand into his. Todd pulled her close, and they fell easily into step, swaying in time to the music. When Elizabeth rested her head on Todd's shoulder, he was intoxicated by the sweet scent of her hair.

Todd clasped Elizabeth's slim waist firmly, his thoughts spinning and whirling much more quickly than the music. *Elizabeth and I fit together like two links in a gold chain. This feels so right, so perfect.* Todd smiled and closed his eyes for a second, letting the world dissolve around him.

Todd stared down at Elizabeth, resisting the temptation to kiss her forehead. *I thought I'd gotten Elizabeth Wakefield out of my system a long time ago. But I had forgotten how good she makes me feel—better than I have in ages.*

The song wound to a halt, fading into a more upbeat, brassy number. "Feel better, Liz?"

Todd asked quietly, not wanting to remove his arm from Elizabeth's waist.

Elizabeth nodded and turned her brightening eyes to his. "Yeah," she said, moving away from him gently. "Yeah, actually, I do."

"Well, then, let's finish our shopping, OK?" Todd smiled mischievously. "Unless we've been banned from the store."

Elizabeth laughed softly and held out her hand. "You lead the way, Todd."

Ah, peace and quiet, Tom said to himself. It felt good to kick back and vegetate after an action-packed evening. After a total of three games of Monopoly, four wrestling matches, and at least thirty tickling fights, Tom was exhausted.

He settled back into the leather recliner and grabbed the stereo remote, switching selections on the CD player. A bluesy ballad floated from the speakers. He put the remote down on the end table next to a photograph in a heavy silver frame. Idly Tom picked it up.

Mr. Conroy and his late wife, Joanne, smiled out at him. Their arms were wrapped around each other, and it was clear that they had been completely, happily in love. Tom remembered the tears that came to Mr. Conroy's eyes whenever he talked about his wife. "No one can replace Joanne," he had said.

The memory brought with it a wave of resentment. *How could Elizabeth slander such a good man's name? George wouldn't even look at another woman, let alone a much younger one who happened to be dating his own son.* He slammed the picture frame down on the table. *Lies, total lies. Elizabeth doesn't care how much she hurt us. She—*

"Hi, son," Mr. Conroy said cheerily, his deep voice breaking through Tom's anger. "I hope it's not too late. Did those little hooligans of mine wear you out?"

"Are you kidding? Iron Man Watts, knocked out by a couple of kids?" Tom groaned dramatically. "Of course they killed me. I feel like an old, old man."

"Well, you don't look like one." Mr. Conroy loosened his tie, removed his suit jacket, and sank into a plush chair. "Tom, you're way too young and good-looking to be wasting your Friday nights baby-sitting. I'm grateful you could do it this time, but—"

"What?" Tom shifted uneasily in his seat. The expression on his father's face warned him he wasn't going to like this conversation.

"I was wondering . . . have you spoken to Elizabeth lately?"

Tom shook his head. "No, and I really don't want to discuss her right now."

Mr. Conroy held up a hand. "I know, I know. You're still upset. But listen, Tom, maybe Elizabeth was just feeling a little left out. After all, we suddenly popped into your life and very quickly started taking up all of your time. Maybe you talked so much about us that she just couldn't help but become jealous. She's only human." Mr. Conroy's eyes implored him. "Can't you give her a second chance?"

Tom bit his lip, trying to hold back the hot, savage words that threatened to spill out. *I wish you could hear this, Liz. You would be ashamed of yourself. George is willing to forgive you. But I'm not.* "There's a lot more to my troubles with Elizabeth than jealousy and insecurity. I really don't want to go into it right now."

Mr. Conroy nodded. "You're right. I shouldn't interfere. Besides, some relationships just aren't meant to be." The song on the CD faded away, punctuating the silence that fell between them.

"You know, Tom," Mr. Conroy began, "things may be over with Elizabeth, but that doesn't mean you have to become a recluse."

"I know."

"A handsome, charming, bright young man like yourself shouldn't be alone," Mr. Conroy continued.

"George, maybe I should let *you* find dates

for me. You have an amazing way with words."

Mr. Conroy chuckled and got to his feet. "I've got to get out of these stuffy clothes," he said, scooping up his jacket and tie. "You don't need my help, Tom. Just remember this, though. I know it's not an original thought, but there are plenty of other fish in the sea."

Tom watched Mr. Conroy admiringly as he left the den. *Maybe George is right. No, there's no maybe about it. He is right. There are lots of fish in the sea—and it's time for me to cast my net.*

Why does Todd have that weird look on his face? Elizabeth wondered as she opened the door to Dickenson Hall. *And why am I letting him follow me home and carry my groceries?* Elizabeth shot Todd a tense look over her shoulder as they made their way up to the room Elizabeth shared with her twin sister.

"Liz, I'm so glad I ran into you tonight," Todd said brightly.

"Um . . ." Elizabeth stalled, not knowing what to say. Todd seemed too eager, too cheerful. Between the kisses in Todd's dorm and the dancing in the mall parking lot, things seemed to be getting a little out of hand. The whole situation was making Elizabeth nervous all over again.

"And thanks for inviting me up too," Todd added quickly.

But I didn't invite you—you invited yourself, Elizabeth argued silently as the elevator doors opened. "That's OK. I could use the help." *No, I couldn't. But what could I do? Say no?*

Elizabeth was relieved it was a Friday night, so the dorm was empty. Elizabeth could just imagine all the surprised looks if people saw her strolling in with Todd. She knew they must look incredibly domestic, with Todd toting her groceries.

Todd whistled "Yesterday" softly, his face a picture of blissful contentment. Unease shot through Elizabeth's veins. She had to straighten things out—*now.*

When they reached her door, Elizabeth held out her arms for the groceries. "Thanks, Todd, I can take it from here," she said gently as possible.

Todd handed her the bags, but his face fell. "I don't understand—"

"I know I probably sound like an ungrateful jerk, but I just need to spend some time alone right now."

"Sure, Liz. I don't want to bother you," he answered in a low voice. But Todd's brown eyes turned so dark and intense that Elizabeth dropped her grocery bags.

"Todd, what's going on?" Elizabeth demanded, immediately regretting it. She didn't mean to blurt it out quite that boldly, but Todd's look triggered an impulse she couldn't control.

He raised his brows innocently. "I just wanted to help—"

"I mean, what do you want from me?" Elizabeth bit her lip nervously and unsuccessfully willed her heart to slow down.

"*Nothing*, Liz. Why are you so defensive? Did I do something to make you upset again?" Todd asked gently.

Elizabeth's heart was now speeding like a racehorse's. She put her hand to her sizzling hot forehead, knowing she had just made a prize fool out of herself. "No, I'm sorry; it's just . . . oh, forget it."

"No, Liz, I won't." Todd ran his fingers nervously through his hair. "Come on, you've got to be straight with me. Is this about last week? Is this about what happened between us? Because if it is—"

Elizabeth raised a hand to stop him. "I *really* don't want to discuss that right now. Let's just call it a night, OK?" Turning around, she swept up the bags of groceries and grabbed the doorknob in a single, seamless gesture. "Good night, Todd," she said to the door.

"Wait, Liz," Todd began, "don't go just yet. I want to know—"

"Please," she begged, "let's just call it a night. I can't think right now."

"But—"

"Good night, Todd," she said again, softly but firmly, as she let herself into the room and swiftly shut the door behind her.

"I can't believe what that man did to me!" Jessica screeched to the ceiling. She made a quick circuit around the room before scooping up a pillow and hurling it violently at the wall. It hit its mark with a satisfying thud. Her mind blazed with questions. *How could Nick not invite me to dinner tomorrow? Do I embarrass him? Does he think his parents won't approve of me?*

"Argh!" Jessica pounded her fist on her bed, shoving aside the heaps of clothing and books so she could flop down on it. "Nick is *so* inconsiderate and *so* mean," she proclaimed to a teddy bear that was half covered by an old sweatshirt. "He is *sooo* cold and *sooo* arrogant. How can he treat me like this?" She raised her eyes to the ceiling. *"How!"* She threw another pillow across the room for emphasis.

"Jessica, what on earth is going on?"

Jessica whirled around and faced Elizabeth, who stood gaping at her from the doorway as she slowly let her bags slide to the floor.

"Hi, Liz," Jessica said automatically before launching back into her tirade. "Nick Fox is the most infuriating man! He's never around when I need him—*never!* And now he's booked an

34

entire Saturday night so he can have dinner with his parents!"

"His parents? What's wrong with that?" Elizabeth asked disinterestedly as she turned and walked toward the kitchenette.

"Listen, will you?" Jessica followed close on her sister's heels. "I'm trying to tell you something important!"

Elizabeth didn't respond; she just started putting away groceries as if she had no idea her poor sister was enduring a major crisis. Jessica put her hands on her hips and flung her hair out of her eyes. *What is wrong with her?* Jessica wondered. *She's acting like a space cadet or something. Doesn't she care about* my *pain and anguish?* Jessica glared at her twin. *Sometimes Liz can be so self-absorbed.* "Liz, will you pay attention—"

Elizabeth looked up from a box of what appeared to be fruit-filled cookies and stared blankly at Jessica for a second. Finally her aquamarine eyes focused and grew sharp. "I can't handle this right now, Jessica. I have a lot on my mind."

Jessica narrowed her eyes at her sister. "Well, *pardonnez-moi.* I can see that your box of cookies is much more important to you. It's not like I'm your only sister or anything." She waited for a heated retort, but none came. *This is too much,* she realized silently. *Elizabeth is totally freaking me out.*

"Earth to Elizabeth," Jessica said in a loud, sarcastic tone. "Houston, do we have contact?"

Elizabeth frowned at her and slammed the box of cookies down on top of the microwave—hard. "I heard you. How could I *not* hear you?" Elizabeth stormed over to her immaculately made bed and sank down on it as Jessica flopped back onto her own.

Elizabeth briefly covered her face with her hands before looking up. "For your information, those were sugar-free fruit bars, not cookies," she said.

"Oh, great, I feel *so* much better. Now that I know there's no sugar in your cookies—excuse me—*fruit bars,* I can sleep easy tonight. Thanks a *lot* for ignoring me in my time of need, Liz." Jessica was careful to coat each word in a thick layer of sarcasm. But Elizabeth didn't respond; she didn't even move or blink. Jessica was momentarily tempted to walk over and take her sister's pulse, but her thoughts flew back to Nick.

He'd better call me, like in ten minutes, or he's toast, she thought furiously. Her feet hurt from her wild race across the beach, and then she had to spend her last few dollars on a taxi ride home. But what else could she have done? There was no way she'd allow Nick Fox to take her home after he'd so deeply insulted her.

Jessica had opened her mouth to launch into yet another tirade when there was a knock at the door. Elizabeth remained frozen in place, so Jessica sprang up, marched to the door, and yanked it open.

Her jaw dropped as she saw who was standing there. *Todd Wilkins?* Before Jessica could utter a word, another head popped up right behind Todd's. *Nick!* Suddenly all Jessica's fury was replaced with a warm feeling of satisfaction. Or maybe it was just plain gloating. *There'd better be flowers hidden behind Nick's back. Or better yet,* diamonds.

Todd was waving something at her while Nick waited patiently behind him, his pine green eyes quizzical. "I took Elizabeth's grocery receipt by accident," Todd said. "I—uh—is she here?"

Jessica snatched the receipt from his hand. "Sorry, she's in the shower." She reached around Todd and grabbed Nick's arm. "*We* have to talk," she said significantly to Nick, then turned to give Todd a pointed look. "See you later, Todd. I'll tell Elizabeth you stopped by."

As Todd wandered off, Nick asked, "Is he all right? He looked kind of out of it."

"Never mind him," Jessica snapped, and led Nick into the room. "We have more pressing matters to discuss."

Nick glanced at Elizabeth, who was sitting still as a statue on her bed. He turned to Jessica with one of his you're-up-to-something looks. "I thought you said your sister was in the shower, Jess."

Jessica tossed her head while Elizabeth woke from her trance. "What? What shower? What's going on?"

Jessica rolled her eyes. "I did you a favor, silly."

"What *favor?*" Elizabeth asked in a rising tone.

"Todd Wilkins was here, and I got rid of him for you. I told him you were in the shower. Pretty clever, eh?"

"Jessica, you lied!" Elizabeth squealed. "I can't believe you."

"Well, honestly, Liz, did you *really* want to see *Todd?*"

"Well, no," Elizabeth admitted sheepishly. "Not really. I need some time alone right now."

"There! You see, I *did* do you a favor after all!" Jessica crowed, shooting a triumphant look at Nick. "Have a seat," she commanded, gesturing to her wildly messy bed. When Nick didn't move, she shoved everything onto the floor and gave Nick a little push. "We have to talk, Nick," she demanded, directing a fierce look at her twin.

Elizabeth seemed to get the message. *At least my sister is a quick study,* Jessica thought cheerfully, *even if she does seem mixed up about her love life.* What the heck *was* going on with Elizabeth and Todd? Jessica gave herself a mental shake. *Not my problem,* she reminded herself. *Not now, at least.*

Elizabeth sighed heavily. "I guess I'll go for a walk or something." She threw Jessica a martyred look.

Jessica walked to the closet and took out a towel and a shower cap. "Or you could take a shower after all, and then it won't be a lie." She widened her eyes innocently and smothered a grin as her sister angrily snatched the items from her outstretched hands.

"Fine," Elizabeth snarled, "and I suppose you want me to make it a long one." She stomped toward the door and jerked it open.

"Make it a *very* long one," Jessica called after her. She giggled and shook her head. *Liz can be such a trip sometimes,* she thought smugly. *Teasing her is too much fun.* Jessica sat next to Nick and turned toward him expectantly. "Well?" she asked, crossing her arms in front of her.

Nick reached for Jessica's hand. "Jess, I've come to say I'm sorry." He brushed his thick brown hair from his eyes.

I love it when he does that, Jessica thought. *His hair is so perfect—not deadbeat long, but not frat-boy short either.* Since Nick wasn't working undercover at the moment, he could afford to

39

look a little more respectable. But even though he'd trimmed his hair a bit and started shaving a little closer, he still had a dangerous edge.

Nick lifted Jessica's hand to his lips and kissed it. "Jessica, believe me, you're not the problem here. I was only trying to explain that my parents are a little, you know, different. Everything has to be just right. I want to make sure that nothing will happen to upset *you*." He paused to stroke his finger along her cheekbone. "Am I forgiven?"

Jessica's anger had deflated faster than a pinpricked balloon. "OK." Jessica fell into Nick's outstretched arms, allowing him to pull her close. His hard, muscled chest rose and fell beneath her cheek. For a long moment she basked in her contentment, drinking in the spicy scent of his aftershave. But there was still one thing she wasn't sure of. Jessica put on the sweetest smile she could muster and looked up at Nick's chiseled face. "Oh, Nick?"

"Mm-hmm?"

"You *do* want me to come along tomorrow night, right?"

Nick groaned and fell back on Jessica's bed in frustration. "Weren't you listening to me, Jessica? I *do* want you to meet my parents, but I need to plan this *carefully*."

Jessica was on the verge of tearing her hair out. But then she made a silent vow to do Nick's hair before starting on her own. "You didn't answer me, Nick! Am I invited or not?"

"The answer is *no,* Jessica," Nick said, sitting up and holding his hands out to her in a pleading gesture. "I know how much you hate to hear that word, but I can't get through to you any other way."

Jessica pouted. "I don't see what the big deal is. If you're not ashamed of me, then why can't I come along?"

"Because my parents will expect us to already be engaged or something. Trust me, they'll drive us crazy with questions. Who needs the headache?" Nick explained impatiently.

"So what? We can handle it," Jessica retorted, tossing her head. "I mean, we're a couple, right? And we *are* serious, aren't we? Or are you just pretending?"

Nick threw up his hands. "I give up. *Yes,* Jessica, we are serious, and *no,* I'm not pretending." He affectionately ruffled her hair as a reluctant smile spread across his face. "You're even more persistent than my mother. OK, Jess, we'll *all* have dinner together tomorrow night. Are you satisfied?"

"Almost," she purred, cuddling up against his shoulder.

"Almost!" Nick cried. "What else do you need?"

"This," she whispered, covering his lips with hers.

Chapter Three

Talk about mood swings, Todd thought glumly. He felt as if he were hog-tied upside down on a roller coaster that was going a hundred miles an hour. And the person holding the rope in her dainty little hands was Elizabeth Wakefield.

The quad had been surprisingly quiet as he walked to his dorm. He guessed that all the excitement must be happening off campus, but not even a hundred parties could take his mind off Elizabeth tonight.

I just don't get it, Todd mused, shaking his head. The two of them had really connected in the parking lot—hadn't they? Didn't Elizabeth feel the same way he did?

As Todd dug his keys out of his pocket, the telephone inside his room began to ring. *That's her!* Eagerly Todd fumbled with the doorknob and wanted to kick himself for using the wrong key. Anxiety made his hands damp and clumsy as he fumbled with his key ring. After what seemed like an eternity, he finally found the right key.

Thrusting open the door, he fell into the room and lunged for the telephone all in one motion. He wasn't a top athlete for nothing. "Hello?" he asked expectantly.

"Todd? Is that you? I can barely hear you." *Gin-Yung.* Todd's heart dropped like a fifty-pound barbell.

"Todd? Todd, are you there?" Gin-Yung's voice sounded hesitant and far away.

He held the phone tighter with trembling, slippery hands. "Sure, I'm here. It's great to hear your voice," Todd said, hoping he didn't sound fake. As he grabbed a nearby chair he realized he couldn't think of anything to talk about.

"You sound kind of weird. Are you OK? You're not sick or anything, are you?" The faint crackling of the long-distance call did nothing to hide the concern in Gin-Yung's voice.

Todd cleared his throat loudly. "I'm OK, Gin-Yung. What's going on?"

"Not much. I've been feeling kind of dragged out lately."

"Knowing you, you're working too hard," Todd said as good-naturedly as possible. "You should take it easy. No more of this overachiever business."

"I don't know. I think my get-up-and-go has got up and gone." She laughed a little. "Don't worry about me. Maybe I need to take some vitamins or something."

"Good idea. You should try E and some megavitamins," he said quickly, feeling his face burn. The timing of the call and her mention of vitamins were enough to make Todd believe Gin-Yung might actually know something about his rendezvous with Elizabeth at the Organic Palace. *Don't be an idiot,* he scolded himself. *No one was around to call her and tell her about it. And if Gin-Yung were psychic, you would know that by now.* An image of Gin-Yung waving her hands around a crystal ball popped into his head.

"What, Todd?"

"Huh?"

"You sounded like you were laughing." Gin-Yung's voice didn't sound as sharply inquisitive as Todd would have expected. She just sounded tired.

"Wasn't me," Todd said, cursing himself. "Maybe we're getting our lines crossed or something."

"Maybe." She took a pause and sighed. "I miss you, Todd. London is exciting and everything, but I really miss you."

"Me too," he whispered into the receiver. He couldn't *not* say it, after all. Not with Gin-Yung sounding so forlorn. "I should probably let you go. This call is costing you a fortune."

"I guess you're right," she said softly. "Talk to you later, OK?"

After they said good-bye, Todd hung up the phone and stared at it for a long, agonized moment. He felt like a complete jerk, but he couldn't help it if the conversation was a stiff one. He and Gin-Yung had drifted apart, plain and simple.

We agreed to see other people, he reminded himself, *so it's not like I would be sneaking around behind her back. And I never promised to sit home alone every night.*

Sighing loudly, he reached for his basketball. He twirled it expertly on one finger as he stared off into space.

There's nothing to feel guilty about here, he told himself. *I just happen to need a social life, and I just happen to want Elizabeth to be a part of it.*

"Come on, Tom, you can stay a little longer. *Pleeease?*" Jake whined, hanging tightly on to Tom's left arm. Jake blocked the front door of Mr. Conroy's condo, puffing up like a miniature muscle man.

"Sorry, guy," Tom said, shaking Jake free so that he could pick up his overnight bag. "But the beds here are too comfortable for my own good. I slept too long, ate too much, and now I'm way too late."

Jake held out his arms. "Swing me around again first. Pleeease?"

Tom couldn't resist. With his bag slung over his shoulder, Tom picked up his little half brother and swung him for what must have been the fifteenth time that morning.

Jake let out a whoop. "You're the Incredible Hulk, Tom. I bet *no one* is as strong as you." Tom spun him around faster. "Hey, guys!" Jake shouted. "Look at me!"

"We see you, son." Mr. Conroy chuckled. He was lounging on the settee in the entryway. "You better let your big brother go, though. He has things to do."

Carefully Tom set Jake down. "The Incredible Hulk, huh? I don't know if that's a compliment or not, Jake."

"Can't you stay, Tom?" Mary asked wistfully. "You can have lunch with us. We'll eat anything you want."

Tom reached over and gently tugged Mary's long blond hair. "Hey, after all those pancakes I don't think I'll be able to eat until tomorrow! Besides, I promised my friend Danny I'd go running with him." He patted his flat stomach. "I'm so weighed down, I'll barely be able to walk, let alone jog."

"Maybe if we feed you more, you'll have to stay with us," Mary suggested. "Then if you wanted to leave, we'd have to roll you out."

Tom laughed. "Actually that doesn't sound too bad. But since I'm able to walk on my own right now, I'd better open that door and do it."

After everyone said their good-byes, Tom rushed out the front door and shut it behind him. He nearly tripped over someone standing directly in his path.

Tom quickly recovered his balance and reached out to stop the dark-haired woman from falling. "Hey, I'm sorry," he said, steadying her. "Are you OK?"

He looked down and saw that this was no ordinary woman. She was stunning—tall and curvy with glossy mahogany hair that fell past her shoulders. Her white sleeveless pantsuit showed off her tan perfectly. Doelike hazel eyes locked with Tom's for a long moment. Full, red lips curved in an answering smile.

"I'm fine," the woman said in a low, sultry voice. "I guess I should thank you. You caught me before I could fall." She rang the Conroys' doorbell and glanced back at Tom before the door to the condo opened and she stepped inside.

Tom's face was warm, and his heart thudded like an engine with a too fast idle. *Wow*, he whispered to himself. *Wow*.

He wandered out to the parking lot in a daze. Slipping into his car, he asked himself out loud, *"Who* was *that?"*

*　　*　　*

"You're out of your mind, Lila," Jessica announced calmly. She knew Lila could be pretty weird sometimes, but right now she was amazed at just *how* weird.

"No, I'm not," Lila responded evenly. "There is nothing worse than having a man's mother like you too much." She tossed her impeccable brown hair over one shoulder and reached up to tighten one star sapphire earring. They were real star sapphires, of course. Every item adorning Lila Fowler was expensive and tasteful. It all came with the territory of being born rich and marrying a wealthy Italian count whose unexpected, tragic death would only add to the already enormous Fowler fortune.

The whole world seemed to go shopping on Saturdays, but that never fazed Jessica, Lila, and Isabella Ricci. They were pros when it came to working the corridors of the Sweet Valley Mall, and today's mission was to find the perfect ensemble for Jessica's dinner with the Foxes.

Jessica's forehead crinkled. "I don't get it, Li. How can it be bad if your boyfriend's mother is crazy about you?"

"I've got to admit, Lila. It sounds weird to me too." Isabella raised one flawless brow quizzically.

"Think about it. Do you really want a man's

mother to be more thrilled with you than *he* is?" Lila looked from Jessica to Isabella, as if she was daring them to say yes. "No, you don't. I should know."

"Uh-oh," Isabella quipped, fixing her luminous gray eyes on Jessica's eyes. "I think I feel a story coming on."

"Listen, you guys," Lila began, seeming to ignore Isabella completely. "I dated Kipper Ellington while I was vacationing in Aruba."

"Kipper?" Jessica giggled. "Don't tell me that's his real name, Lila." She met Isabella's amused gaze and giggled even harder.

"Well, it was," Lila snapped. "Will you pay attention? I haven't gotten to the important part yet."

"OK, OK," Jessica said quickly, holding up a hand appeasingly. "Please tell us more about *Kipper*."

Lila rolled her eyes. "Kipper seemed like he had it all. He was gorgeous, drove a hot car, went to the best prep school, and knew his way around the country club scene. Plus he was crazy about me. I mean, like he wouldn't be, right? Anyway, it was absolutely perfect until I met his mother. Now, Popsy Ellington—"

"Popsy?" Jessica was on the verge of losing it completely.

"Makes perfect sense to me," Isabella said,

flipping her jet-black hair over her shoulder and holding her lips together tightly.

Jessica took one look at Isabella's face and the two of them burst into sputtering laughter. They had to hold on to each other to keep from falling over.

Lila came to a dead stop and tapped her foot impatiently, eyes narrowed. "Get a grip. I'm just trying to give you a little warning, Jess."

"Fire away, Li," Jessica said, trying desperately to maintain her composure. She decided to focus on one of Lila's earrings. If she took one more look at Isabella, she knew she'd be a goner.

"Mrs. Ellington immediately made this huge fuss over me. First she insisted I call her Popsy. Then she told me she always wanted to have a daughter just like me."

"That doesn't sound so bad," Isabella said.

"Is-a-*bella*, the woman already had three daughters and a daughter-in-law."

"Well, OK, maybe that's a little strange," Isabella agreed.

"And that wasn't all of it. By the time tea was served, Mrs. Ellington had told me about all the plans she had laid out for Kipper—and *me!* She was having a house built for us, and had hired an interior designer and a landscape artist and everything. Then she dragged out all these catalogs and sample books to ask me which wallpaper pattern or silver setting I preferred. And this was after only *three* dates!" Lila shuddered.

Lila can be so inconsiderate, Jessica thought. *I ask for a little advice and she gives me a bad soap opera plot. Thanks a whole lot, Li.*

Lila continued. "It was like they were planning one of those arranged marriages or something. I felt so trapped. Even though it was totally rude of me, I booked a flight back to Sweet Valley the next day without even saying good-bye. I'm surprised they haven't tried to track me down."

"Boy, that is pretty bizarre," Isabella said.

"That's why I never told anyone about it before."

"No wonder." Jessica snickered. "I'd want to keep Kipper and Popsy a secret too."

Lila responded by pointing out a small, exclusive boutique at the end of one hall. "Why don't we look in Chantal's Collections, Jessica?" she asked sweetly.

"Not today," Jessica answered, seething. Lila knew darn well Jessica could hardly afford to even walk past the boutique, let alone shop there.

"Oh, well, there's always Up and Coming." Lila groaned.

"Good choice," Isabella said. "I've found gorgeous stuff there for practically nothing."

"OK," Jessica said, casting a longing look

toward Chantal's Collections before following her friends into Up and Coming. They were instantly bombarded with Top-Forty music and the overwhelming aroma of rose potpourri.

Jessica grabbed a shiny red full-length jacket out of Lila's hands and put it on. She smiled at her reflection in the huge floor-length mirror. *I'm so lucky,* she thought. *I look good in any color.*

"You can't be serious, Jessica," Lila demanded huffily.

"Nope," she replied, taking off the jacket and handing it back to Lila. "I have to look absolutely perfect for Nick and his folks tonight."

Isabella patted her arm. "You'll do fine. Don't worry."

Lila slipped on a pair of sunglasses. "But you *must* be nervous, Jessica. After all, Nick is one hot guy. You don't want to blow it."

"Gee, thanks, Li. I needed that. At least Izzy's trying to help me out here." Jessica mustered up a confident smile. "Anyway, I know Nick's parents will love me. I mean, how could they not?" She preened in front of the mirror and held up an off-white, very short skirt.

"I bet they couldn't if you wore something like *that*." Lila pointed at the skirt Jessica was holding.

"Puh-*leeze*, Lila. Like I would really wear something like this to meet the Foxes." Jessica bit her lip as she put the skirt back on the rack. "I have to look gorgeous and elegant, but not too much, you know what I mean?"

"Exactly," Lila said, nodding. "You have to do everything you can to make tonight perfect. And then, who knows? Maybe even that won't be enough. As a rule, you should remember that your boyfriend's parents are usually the most difficult people in the world to impress."

Jessica snorted. "Thanks a lot, Lila. I could really use a lot more of your help."

"You know, my first dinner with Danny's parents *did* almost turn into a disaster," Isabella began. "The first thing I did was spill red wine all over the white linen tablecloth."

Lila gasped. "You must have wanted to die."

"Well, almost." Isabella rolled her eyes. "But that's not all. When I was handing a dish to Mrs. Wyatt, my bracelet hooked on to the sleeve of her silk dress. It snagged."

"And Danny's *still* allowed to date you?" Lila looked amazed.

"Actually the evening ended pretty well. I got to be really friendly with the Wyatts. Plus the whole ordeal brought Danny and me even closer together."

"Thank goodness," Jessica exclaimed. "I don't think I could take another parental horror story." She shot Lila an accusing look.

Lila was busy examining a tangerine shirt-dress. "Didn't Nick tell you his parents were hard to get along with?"

"Hmmm, too plain," Jessica said, shaking her head firmly as Lila held up the dress. "He did say that, but you know how everyone always thinks their parents are the weirdest."

"True," Lila agreed, studying a zippered vest and a black micro-miniskirt.

"That's way too wild, Lila," Jessica protested.

"I know. I'm looking at it for *me*."

Jessica cast her eyes around the store, hoping a spotlight would suddenly beam down from the ceiling and illuminate the perfect outfit. "Look at it this way. Nick adores me, and Nick's parents adore him. *Therefore* Nick's parents will adore me, right?" Just then Jessica caught a glimpse of a pink sleeve peeking out from a rackful of dark clothes. She dashed over and pulled out the hanger, letting out a squeal of joy.

It was perfect. The dress was a shell pink sleeveless shift that fell just a couple of inches above the knee. The matching long-sleeved jacket made the entire outfit demure and flattering. There was only one, and it was just her size. Jessica flagged down Lila and Isabella and triumphantly held out the outfit for their seal of approval.

"Perfect!" Isabella exclaimed. "You've *got* to buy it, Jess. You'll look fantastic."

"Isabella's right. That's a real find." Lila ran her manicured nails against the weave. "I have to say it's a very good knockoff. Of course, if you bought the real thing in Chantal's, you'd have to spend ten times what they're charging you here."

Jessica ignored her and hugged the dress to her chest. "This is a sign," she crowed. "The perfect dress for the perfect evening. Fate's on my side." She smiled at herself in the mirror. "After all, what could go wrong?"

Chapter Four

"Elizabeth? Hello, Liz? Are you there?"

Elizabeth blinked. She gazed blankly across the table at Nina Harper, who was busy waving her hand in front of Elizabeth's face. The cafeteria was noisier than usual, but Elizabeth hadn't noticed until now. *What are all these people doing here on a Saturday at noon?* she thought distractedly. She gazed down at the turkey quesadilla in front of her. *Come to think of it, what is that doing on my plate? I don't even remember buying it.*

"Li-i-i-i-z," Nina repeated patiently.

"W-What?" Elizabeth stammered, meeting Nina's questioning brown eyes. Elizabeth still got a jolt whenever she looked at her best friend. The soft, shoulder-length curls framing Nina's face made her look incredibly sophisticated; her hairdo was a dramatic change from the beaded braids she used to wear.

Nina took a sip of her skim milk and neatly wiped her mouth on a napkin. "You are *definitely* somewhere else today. Let me guess. You're sick and tired of hearing me gab about the Black Student Union, right?"

"Oh no, Nina, sorry. I just zoned out for a second. I'm back now." Elizabeth leaned her chin on her hand and gave Nina the most expectant look she could muster.

"OK. Bryan has come up with this incredible idea," Nina continued, gesturing in front of her with her slender hands. "He wants to contact the other black student associations from all the universities in California and start planning for the next March on Racism. He's trying to go statewide this time around. Just imagine, Liz . . ."

Elizabeth tried to focus on Nina's words, but her mind drifted off. *What made me dance with Todd in the parking lot yesterday?* she wondered. *Things are moving too quickly. The whole situation could get out of hand if I don't watch it.* Elizabeth kept musing as her eyes wandered inexplicably toward Nina's glass of milk.

"Elizabeth," Nina said loudly. "What's going

on, girl? You're making me nervous." Nina's brow wrinkled with curiosity.

Elizabeth felt her face heat up. Nervously she tightened her ponytail and fidgeted in her chair. She hated being rude to anyone and as a rule considered herself to be a good listener. But today she'd failed on both counts. "I'm really sorry, Nina. I know that it's no excuse, but I've got a lot on my mind."

Nina poked at her fruit salad, her eyes never leaving Elizabeth's. "Like . . ."

"It's—it's Todd," Elizabeth finally blurted, watching Nina's eyebrows shoot up. "I'm getting this feeling that something might happen between us . . . something more than just friendship."

"What's the story?" Nina cut a neat chunk of pineapple and popped it into her mouth.

"Well, last week . . . Todd kissed me," Elizabeth admitted, rolling her fork between her fingers and looking down at her quesadilla. "We kissed each other. It was pretty serious."

Nina set down her fork, her eyes wide. "*What*? How come you didn't tell me?"

Elizabeth could feel her face redden. "I wasn't trying to keep it from you, Nina, honest. But . . . I'd been out at a party beforehand, and, well, I wasn't really myself at the time, you know what I mean?"

"'Fraid I do," Nina replied, nodding sympathetically.

"Todd wasn't taking advantage of me or anything; don't get me wrong," Elizabeth continued. "It was completely mutual. But my motives were totally skewed. And now I'm worried about Todd—really worried. It seems like he wants things to keep going. And I—I just don't know how I feel about that."

"Wow," Nina said, pushing her plate away completely. "Are you sure about Todd, Liz? What about Gin-Yung?"

Elizabeth sighed. "They had an agreement to see other people while they're apart. He still cares about her, I know. But there's just this—this *intensity* about him now. And I've known Todd for too long to pretend it's something else." She put her head in her hands and groaned. "I can't believe I let this happen, Nina. What am I going to do?"

Nina studied Elizabeth for a long second. "Do you think this is happening because of Tom? Maybe you're still hurting, and it's affecting your judgment."

"Tom?" Elizabeth felt as if every one of her nerve endings had been slashed and left painfully exposed. "You've got to be kidding, Nina! Tom Watts is *not* the issue here. He's out of my life *completely*."

"But you only just broke up. And it was very rough for you," Nina interjected. "You haven't had closure yet. The pain is still fresh. I just don't want you to get hurt, Liz. Jumping from relationship to relationship can really backfire."

"I know you mean well, Nina, but you're wrong. Believe me, I know how I feel about Tom," Elizabeth responded hotly. "Tom Watts showed his true colors. He's selfish, crude, and unfeeling. He's history, Nina. Totally."

"I'm sorry, Liz," Nina answered quietly and evenly. "I didn't mean to upset you." Nina returned to her fruit salad, and a heavy silence fell between them.

Elizabeth blinked back hot tears. Even with Tom Watts out of her life, he was still nothing but trouble. Elizabeth never knew when the pain would start up again. She looked across the table, furious at herself for channeling her angry feelings for Tom toward her best friend.

"Sorry I went off on you, Nina," Elizabeth said quietly.

Nina looked up from her plate and nodded. "That's OK. I'm just nosy, that's all."

"No, you're a good listener, which is something I haven't been all day." Elizabeth paused. "Nina, there's more to it than just the kiss."

61

"A midnight flight to Vegas?" Nina asked, a mischievous smile playing across her face.

"Hardly." Elizabeth giggled. "It's much weirder. Todd and I ran into each other at the Organic Palace last night. We were out in the parking lot, and somehow we ended up . . . dancing."

"Dancing?"

"Slow dancing. It sounds corny, I know. But it made me feel a lot better." Elizabeth looked off to the side and tried to find the right words. "For those few moments I felt . . . safe. Safe and comforted. Todd was really sweet."

Nina gave Elizabeth a level gaze. "I'm sure it was nice, but—"

"But what?"

Nina took a deep breath. "Shouldn't you be more careful? You are on the rebound, you know."

Elizabeth shifted restlessly. "But it's different with Todd. We have a history. It's not like this would be a new relationship. Todd and I—"

"Hi, guys," a cheerful, deep voice interrupted them. "Mind if I join you?"

Elizabeth's heart lurched as she saw Todd approaching their table. She forced a natural smile on her face to hide the shock coursing through her veins. Why was it that Todd appeared whenever she thought about being with him again? Was it fate?

"Well . . . ," Nina began, watching Elizabeth warily.

"Sure, Todd, pull up a chair," Elizabeth finished, her eyes imploring Nina to relax. "We don't mind, do we?"

Todd sat down beside Nina and dropped his tray on the table. Elizabeth grinned as Todd arranged his plate: two hamburgers with dill pickles, a salad, French fries, and an apple. Plus a shake *and* a soda. "I had a great practice session," he explained. "I don't think I missed a single shot." Todd pretended to slam-dunk his apple, a teasing sparkle in his eye. "Besides, I deserve some real food after all that health food I choked down."

Elizabeth laughed and turned to Nina. "You should have seen some of the weird stuff Todd bought at the Organic Palace. It may have been healthful, but it didn't look too appetizing," she explained.

"Excuse me while I dig in," Todd said, grabbing a handful of French fries with enthusiasm.

Nina suddenly rose from her seat. "I hate to eat and run, but I promised Bryan I would work on his rally letter."

Elizabeth smiled brightly. "I'll catch up with you later. Thanks for your advice, Nina. I feel a *lot* better now."

Nina rolled her eyes. "I'm glad, Liz. I really am."

*   *   *

63

Todd nervously turned his can of soda in his hands as he watched Nina disappear into the crowd. He didn't mean to chase her off, but he wasn't a bit sorry to have Elizabeth all to himself. "So, here we are," he began tentatively.

"Yes, indeed," Elizabeth replied, poking at the barely touched quesadilla on her plate.

"Just like the old days, right?" Todd asked, mentally chiding himself for not being able to come up with something even slightly more clever.

But suddenly Elizabeth smiled, and her face reminded Todd of sunshine breaking through clouds. "Funny you should say that," she said cheerfully. "I was just thinking about high school a little while ago. We really had fun back then, didn't we?"

"Absolutely," he agreed eagerly.

"Even when we got into trouble. . . ." Elizabeth looked down, blushing a little.

"Wait a minute; wasn't your sister the one who was always in hot water?"

Elizabeth chuckled. "Hey, if my memory serves me correctly, you were usually willing to help me rescue her."

"Remember Club X—"

Elizabeth groaned and clapped her hand to her forehead. "How could I forget? That group of guys pulling all those stupid pranks. And then Jessica insisted on joining—just to tick Bruce Patman off."

"Yeah, Patman couldn't stand the competition. He was so nervous about Jessica becoming the wildest member of his club. We both tried talking Jess out of joining, but as usual—"

"*—she wouldn't listen,*" Todd and Elizabeth chorused together, shaking their heads in unison.

"I couldn't believe that Jessica would actually go and steal Bruce's car like that. She almost got herself killed, and it was all just to prove a stupid point." Elizabeth sighed deeply. "She really dug herself in deep with Principal Cooper."

"Old Chrome Dome," Todd said fondly.

"Come on, he was a good principal," she added, looking up at him through her lashes. "How come Jessica's messes always ended up being *ours*? Remember how we got into a huge fight when I had to take a test in Jessica's place because instead of studying, she was sneaking around with that college guy—"

"Scott Daniels!" Todd finished for her. "You weren't ready for her test and wound up failing it. And Jessica ended up with a bad case of poison ivy." He stirred his shake slowly with the straw. "Her little schemes always seemed to blow up in her face."

"I'll say. But then again, so did some of mine. Remember Operation Pair Up, when I tried to get Dana and Aaron together?" Elizabeth rolled her eyes. "You tried to convince me not to meddle, and you were right."

"Jeez, that was a mess," Todd remembered. "By the time your plan took off, no one was even speaking anymore."

"But it ended up OK. Dana and Aaron got together, and we made up." Elizabeth looked away for a quiet moment, then gave Todd a shy smile. "You know, I was just thinking about Secca Lake—how we used to sit at our favorite spot and talk."

Todd felt warmth flow through him. "I remember the kisses too."

Elizabeth's face reddened even more. *Is she remembering last week?* Todd wondered. *I know I am.* Those kisses were burned into his brain. When Elizabeth's lips touched his, he felt as though he was flying back in time, back to the best days of his life. The days he had spent with Elizabeth.

"What happened to us, Liz?" Todd blurted impulsively. "How could I let you slip out of my life?"

Elizabeth raised her eyes and aimed a level look at him. She didn't say a word, but the crushing sadness reflected in her blue-green eyes reminded him of the answer he knew all too well. It had been his fault. Todd lost Elizabeth because he was a selfish, arrogant jerk who wanted more from Elizabeth than she was willing to give.

When he first arrived at SVU, Todd thought he had it all. He was a hotshot player for the Sweet Valley University basketball team, a campus celebrity who demanded—and got—attention everywhere he went. He was so intent on playing the role of BMOC that he'd tried pressuring Elizabeth into taking their relationship to a more physical level.

Elizabeth told me she wasn't ready to take that step, but I thought I was. Todd winced at the memory. *She told me no, so I simply left her and replaced her with someone else. I ended up losing my virginity to Lauren Hill, who's faded out of my life completely. I didn't even love her.*

"I'm so sorry, Elizabeth," Todd said urgently. "About everything. I can't even begin to tell you how sorry."

Elizabeth said nothing. Her jaw remained tightened, her shoulders stiff.

"My biggest regret is how I treated you. I'd never do anything like that again, Elizabeth. Not to you or to anyone."

She sighed. "Oh, Todd . . ."

"No, really. I was a monster." He gave her a pleading look. "I've changed, though. I learned my lesson the hard way."

"I know," Elizabeth began.

"You don't, though. I admit I had to take a licking first, but I finally got the message. I thought I was a big man, but what I really needed to do was grow up." Todd ran a hand through his thick dark hair. "I've learned what respect is really all about, Liz. I just wish I could go back in time and fix everything."

"Todd . . ." Some of the rigidity in her face melted. "Maybe we each had to go through hard times before we learned our lessons. It was rough at first, but I think it's made us both a lot stronger."

Todd ached to put his arms around her, but her slender shoulders still looked tense. *I want to make it up to you, Liz,* he pleaded silently. *Please give me a chance. Please give me a sign at least.*

Elizabeth looked up, and her tiny smile made Todd's heart pound uncontrollably. *It's destiny,* he decided. *Elizabeth and I were meant to be together.*

"Where are all the gorgeous women on this campus?" Tom demanded as he jogged down the SVU pedestrian path. He moved smoothly, his legs strong and his body alive and energized.

Danny Wyatt shot his roommate a surprised look as he ran beside him. "Hey, I thought you were taking a hiatus from romance."

Tom shook his head. "Not anymore. I've been totally rejuvenated. No more of that one-on-one stuff, Danny. I learned my lesson. I'm too young to be tied down."

For a brief second Danny's handsome brow creased with concern. Then he shrugged and patted Tom on the back. "Whatever floats your boat, Watts. It's just good to see you so upbeat. Man, you've been a regular old grizzly these last few days."

Tom shook his head. "I know. But I've put that all behind me. From now on, you count on *me* to cheer *you* up."

"Why the sudden change of heart?" Danny asked.

"It suddenly occurred to me. I'm young. I'm single. Why am I wasting my time hiding out? There's a great big world out there, full of people. Full of beautiful, exciting women."

Danny grinned at him. "Let me guess. You've already met one of these beautiful, exciting women?"

Tom remembered the gorgeous brunette he'd literally bumped into as he left the

Conroys'. "I've seen some likely candidates."

"Knowing you, Watts, you'll have them lining up at the door." Danny gave Tom a light punch on the shoulder.

"You know, I haven't been to a *real* party in ages." Tom wasn't looking for something like the innocent little birthday party Elizabeth threw for him when they were still a couple. No, what he had in mind was a total blowout—the kind of party where the fun never stopped. Loud music, willing women, and absolutely no worries. The kind of bash he would preside over back when he was Wildman Watts, the number-one party animal in the history of Sweet Valley University.

"It sounds like your father's been a good influence," Danny said as they cut across the grass and moved toward the quad.

"George gave it to me straight. He really showed me that it's time for me to make some changes." Tom's dark eyes were serious as they briefly connected with Danny's. "As a matter of fact, I've been thinking about playing football again. For real."

Danny's eyebrows shot up. "Are you serious?"

"Why, don't you think it's a good idea?" Tom asked hesitantly.

"Sure, it is. The team would kill to have you back." Danny paused and took a deep breath.

70

"If you're sure that's what you want."

"I don't know, but I *am* sure that I'm ready to have a good time for once. I can't remember the last time . . ." Suddenly Tom saw something that sent shock waves through his body. His lungs felt as though they had shut down, briefly cutting off his breath. His heart froze inside his chest. Then Tom did a rare thing—he stumbled.

About fifteen feet away Todd Wilkins was leaving the cafeteria with Elizabeth on his arm. They looked too close for words. The sight made Tom's face tingle sharply, almost as though he were reliving the awful moment when Elizabeth slapped him during the argument that led to their breakup.

Tom caught Elizabeth looking over at him and was viciously pleased to see her go pale, her mouth forming a startled *O*. Todd's face hardened as he moved protectively toward Elizabeth.

Liz is sure a fast worker, Tom taunted himself. *Either that, or she had Wilkins waiting in the wings before you even broke up. Maybe that's why she made up those stories about George— they were just an excuse to dump you and hook up with Wilkins again.*

Ignoring Danny's anxiously waving arms, Tom slowed down and walked right over to the couple. Before he could stop himself,

Tom felt his mouth curl into a cruel grin. "I'd be careful if I were you, Wilkins," he spat. "Your little friend here has a big problem with telling the truth. She's nothing but a liar. And if you don't watch your back, she'll put a knife in it."

A tiny, weak moan escaped from Elizabeth's lips. Todd's hands clenched into fists.

Tom absorbed their reactions with wicked glee, using them as encouragement to keep talking. "She may look sweet and innocent, Wilkins, but Elizabeth Wakefield is *poison*."

Tom opened his mouth to say more, but he lost his breath as he felt himself being dragged away.

"What's wrong with you, Watts?" Danny asked softly when he finally let go of him.

If Todd called after him, Tom didn't hear it. He just started jogging again, relieved that Danny wasn't asking any more questions. A sharp pang tore through his heart, but Tom chalked it up to strenuous exercise. He found it hard to swallow, but he was probably just thirsty. *I'm not sorry for what I said,* Tom said silently. *I'm not.*

He had only been telling the truth. Elizabeth Wakefield *was* poison. Even a jerk like Wilkins needed to be warned about her. No, Tom wasn't sorry at all for what he said. His chest swelled with pride and satisfaction as he remembered the stricken look on Elizabeth's face—betrayal and devastation were written there so clearly, so precisely. He'd totally crushed her.

I'm glad I told Elizabeth off, Tom told himself. *Elizabeth doesn't deserve to feel happy. She should be as miserable as I am.*

"That was totally unforgivable," Elizabeth whispered, her words barely passing through her painfully constricted throat. *How could a man I once loved just rip me to pieces like that?* she asked herself as the echoes of Tom's hateful words stabbed into her like red-hot needles.

"Tom Watts is downright vicious," she continued, distractedly brushing wisps of hair from her face. *But you have to face reality, Elizabeth,* she told herself. *No matter how much it hurts.* "I guess he's finally revealing his true self."

"Don't let him get to you, Liz," Todd said strongly.

Elizabeth pulled away and chewed her lip. Blood pounded in her temples as she felt herself getting more and more worked up. "You know, from the way Tom acted right now, you'd never believe that *he* was the one who trashed our relationship."

Elizabeth quickened her pace, her blond ponytail bouncing with each angry step. Hurt developed into intense anger. *Tom has no right to talk about me like that,* Elizabeth fumed. *He has no right.*

Todd halted in his tracks and grasped Elizabeth's shoulder gently. "I know Tom said some awful things, Liz, but you shouldn't let him upset you like this."

Elizabeth tightened her jaw and lifted her chin. "I wish that was possible, Todd," she retorted. "But I don't appreciate being treated like dirt."

Todd nodded, his eyebrows knitted in thought. "Maybe I should have gone after him . . . maybe I should have punched him."

"No, Todd, he's not worth it," Elizabeth declared, hot tears stinging her eyes.

Todd approached her tentatively. "Liz, I'm wondering—"

"What?" Elizabeth snapped, recognizing the hesitation in Todd's voice. She knew he was about to ask a question she didn't want to hear.

"Well, if you're over Watts, why are you so emotional right now?" Todd's eyes were intense, vulnerable. "Are your feelings for him still that strong?"

I wish I knew, Elizabeth thought miserably. She wanted to say the word *no* more than anything. But deep down, in spite of all the pain Tom had put her through, she couldn't say her feelings for him were gone.

Elizabeth slowly met Todd's gaze. "I'm sorry, Todd. . . ." She trailed off when she saw

Todd's shoulders sink down. *I wish I could just tell Todd what I think he wants to hear. But I can't mislead him. He deserves at least that much from me.*

Elizabeth touched Todd's arm gently. "Please try and understand. I'm just so confused right now. I wish I could explain, but . . . but I really don't know what I'm feeling anymore."

Todd nodded slowly, reluctantly. The sun shone on his thick brown hair, casting shadows across his crestfallen, gentle face. "I'm glad you're being honest with me, Liz. I guess I can't ask for more."

Elizabeth's breath caught in her throat when Todd turned his forlorn eyes to hers. She managed a weak smile and was thankful to see him return it. The last thing she wanted was to make Todd feel as upset as she did.

Todd took a deep breath. "Whew—we've been so serious, I think we could use a break."

"You're telling me," Elizabeth said, more than happy to move on to a different subject. "There are times when I wish I could shut my mind off completely."

"Great idea," Todd replied, looking as if he just remembered something. "You know what? I heard they're showing some Laurel and Hardy shorts over at the old-movie theater tonight. And a good slapstick comedy can take your mind off just about anything. Want to go?"

"Absolutely. That's *exactly* what I need." The tightness in Elizabeth's chest eased, and she felt her defenses relax a bit. "Todd, I may be totally mixed up at the moment, but I want you to know that if there's one thing I'm sure of, it's that I'm really glad to have you around right now."

Todd caught her hand and held it. His face brimmed over with such hope that Elizabeth immediately felt a twinge of guilt. *Maybe Nina is right*, she fretted, *maybe I'm just reaching out to Todd for comfort. Maybe I am just on the rebound.*

Chapter
Five

Jessica hit the accelerator and zoomed forward. In one neat maneuver she cut off a lumbering old pickup truck and raced ahead. The truck honked indignantly. Jessica shrugged and flicked back her hair. *Sorry, buddy, but I don't have time to crawl along behind your rusty old heap.* A glance at the digital clock on the dash made her heart pound.

I can't believe I'm late. What will Nick's parents think? What will Nick say? He'll be furious. Jessica frowned worriedly and caught a glimpse of her reflection in the rearview mirror. *At least I look stunning. Maybe that'll make up for my being late.* Her powder pink dress and jacket made the exact impression she was striving for: innocent, but fashionable.

Jessica tapped her glossy pink nails on the

steering wheel impatiently. Now she was behind a giant Cadillac with a grandpa type in a fishing hat at the wheel. Jessica wanted to shriek as the Cadillac slowed down to forty. "Forty on the freeway!" she muttered. "Isn't that illegal or something?" Finally an unexpected gap appeared in the flow of traffic in the left lane— just enough for her to squeeze her Jeep in and pass the boatlike Caddie. Taking a deep breath, she put the pedal to the metal and scooted into the left lane, swerving back in front of the Caddie a microsecond later. At least the grandpa type didn't beep.

Adrenaline raced through Jessica's system. She was actually panting. Driving like a speed demon gave her a major rush. At times like these Jessica usually seized the opportunity to live on the edge and push the envelope like there was no tomorrow. But tonight she wanted to appear reserved and ladylike, even while she was driving by herself in the Jeep. After all, some parents probably didn't appreciate wild-eyed recklessness in their sons' girlfriends.

Anyway, it was *Elizabeth's* fault she was dangerously late and driving like a madwoman. Her lunatic twin had run off on a date with Todd Wilkins before Jessica could ask to borrow her cameo necklace. After a cursory search of

Elizabeth's jewelry box, Jessica wondered if her sister had deliberately hidden it. It had taken Jessica a full extra twenty minutes to find the necklace, wrapped in tissue and tucked away in Elizabeth's lingerie drawer underneath her symmetrically folded slips.

Would Nick and his parents buy that excuse? Jessica ran her tongue over her dry lips and squeezed the steering wheel in frustration. *Honestly. If they want to be mad at someone, it should be Elizabeth!*

Jessica sighed, picturing Nick waiting for her at the door, dressed to the nines with arms outstretched. *What does being a little late matter anyway? Mr. and Mrs. Fox are going to love me,* Jessica decided firmly with a toss of her head. *They won't have a choice. I'll lay on the charm so thick, they won't even know what hit them.*

Suddenly Jessica glanced up and realized her exit was coming—like now! Gasping, she shot across three lanes of traffic, ignoring the chorus of outraged blasts and beeps. She flew down the exit ramp as if it were greased with butter. *Hurry, hurry,* she whispered to herself. *Slow down, slow down,* she pleaded with the clock.

Suddenly a shiny black bumper loomed in front of her. *Oh no*—someone had stopped at the bottom of the ramp. Jessica slammed on her brakes, but not soon enough. The Jeep's tires squealed as she fishtailed into the car ahead of her. The sound of metal kissing metal, the crunch of chrome, made Jessica wince.

Great, she moaned to herself. *This would have to happen* now. She put the car in park, turned on her flashers, and climbed out. Outside, she could see her Jeep was fine, but the spanking new Lexus at the bottom of the ramp hadn't fared so well. Its rear end was bent out of shape a little.

And so was its owner. A middle-aged woman with a face to match her candy apple red suit charged over. "You *idiot!*" she shrieked, shaking her alligator briefcase. "Are you blind or just stupid?"

Jessica had opened her mouth to respond when the woman yelled, "Of all the moronic, pea-brained drivers! You don't deserve to *touch* my Lexus, let alone ram into it like you're playing bumper cars at the county fair!"

Cars backed up behind them in a long snake-like formation. People were shouting out their windows and honking nonstop. Jessica was powerless to stop the tides of hot embarrassment and anger from washing over her. *But the accident isn't my fault,* she reassured herself. *I am totally innocent.*

Jessica steeled herself and crossed her arms with flair. "I hate to break it to you, but if anyone is moronic, it's *you!*" She jabbed her finger indignantly in the woman's face. "*Nobody* stops on a ramp. Was driver's ed too complicated for you?"

The woman's eyes narrowed into slits as she thrust her face toward Jessica's. "Don't you poke your finger at me, peroxide head!"

"Peroxide head?" Jessica put her hands on her hips. "Hel-*lo*-o? This is my natural color, thank you very much. But I guess you have vision trouble. The sign there says *yield*, not *stop!*"

A guy in a delivery truck stuck his head out his window and yelled, "You tell her, girl!"

An older woman in a sedan behind the truck stuck her head out her window and retorted, "Are you kidding? It's that reckless blonde's fault!"

"What are you, nuts?" someone else chimed in. "The Lexus was *asking* to get hit!"

Jessica sucked in a lungful of exhaust-filled air, which left her coughing and sputtering. *How could this night get any worse?* she wondered as she pushed back her hair. Jessica had carefully styled it to fall in a sleek tumble down her back, but now it looked like a bird's nest in a hurricane. A sudden gust of stale air blew Jessica's hair back across her face, nearly driving her to throw a tantrum. As she fought with her wind-blown mane her gaze suddenly fell on the Lexus's vanity plate. Trouble, it read. *Boy, is that the truth*, Jessica thought miserably.

Trouble cleared her throat. "That Jeep of yours sure did a job on my car, considering how accurately it resembles a prize from a box of Cracker Jack."

"You want to talk about toy cars?" retorted Jessica. "Yours looks like it was built for Barbie and Ken!"

The woman moaned and clapped her hand to her forehead before marching over to the rear of her car and studying it. "Well, it's just a little ding, but I'll still want it fixed." She stormed over and gave Jessica a cold look. "Give me your phone number so we can discuss insurance later. I have places to go."

"Fine. So do I," Jessica snapped, rooting through her purse for a paper and pen. "But I'll want your number too."

The woman produced an elegant embossed business card from her briefcase. Jessica threw the card onto the Jeep's dashboard and hastily scribbled her phone number on an old receipt and handed it over. Without another word, Trouble dashed back to her car and finally moved it off the ramp.

Absentmindedly Jessica snatched the woman's card and stuffed it in her purse as she followed the Lexus onto the freeway. When the Lexus turned off at the next exit, she breathed a sigh of relief. *Good. Keep that crazy woman as far away from me as possible,* she thought, driving straight ahead.

While steering with one hand, Jessica peered in the rearview mirror and tried to repair the damage done to her hair and makeup. *At least that nightmare is over and I'm finally on my way,* she assured herself. *This will all be worth it once I meet Nick's parents.*

"Of all the gin joints in all the towns in all the world, she walks into mine. . . ." The rugged face and the sandpaper voice twisted with emotion.

Todd felt an ache of sympathy. *Poor Bogie. Even you fell victim to a beautiful woman. You may have only been acting, but you sure got the agony part of relationships right.*

The Oldies but Goodies Theatre was packed. Obviously there were millions of Bogart and Bergman fans, and it was a Saturday night besides. But for some reason Todd had envisioned that he and Elizabeth would have the theater to themselves. Not that it mattered now. He and Elizabeth could be entirely alone in this dark, cool, intimate place, and it wouldn't have made any difference.

Elizabeth had seemed a little suspicious when the two of them arrived at the theater and saw *Casablanca* on the marquee. But Todd had honestly misread the movie listings; the Laurel and Hardy festival had been the night before. Still, Todd hoped that this turn of events was a sign that the evening would develop into a romantic one. So far that was working only in theory; Todd might as well have been out on a date with his mother.

He stole a look at Elizabeth's delicate profile. She was engrossed, her eyes never moving from the screen. Todd passed her the bucket of popcorn. She dipped her hand in robotically, not seeming to notice what she was doing. *Maybe* Casablanca *wasn't such a hot idea after all,* Todd realized. *Elizabeth is in her own galaxy, and I'm the Invisible Man.*

Todd wriggled uncomfortably in his seat despite the plush cushions. Ingrid Bergman's luminous face filled the screen. When she pouted her full red lips and said, "Kiss me. Kiss me as if it were the last time," Todd shivered at the passion in her voice.

Was this movie giving Elizabeth any ideas? Todd thought of putting his arm around her shoulders but rejected it right away. This wasn't high school, after all. *You'd think I'd be a lot suaver by now*, Todd thought with an inward groan. *Why can't I be more like Bogie? Look at how he handled that other woman in the movie, Yvonne.* When she had asked, "Will I see you tonight?" Humphrey Bogart had answered, "I don't make plans that far ahead."

Bogie was the King of Smooth.

"How many times have you seen this movie, Liz?" Todd whispered optimistically. "I've seen it—"

"Shhh," she hissed softly. Elizabeth didn't even turn to look at him; her eyes were riveted.

Todd sighed and sank back in his seat. *Jeez, this isn't working out at all. I might as well be sitting here alone. All the romantic action is happening up there on the screen. What would Bogie do in a jam like this?*

Todd leaned over and placed his lips close to Elizabeth's ear. "Ingrid Bergman isn't half as beautiful as you are," he murmured.

It seemed to work. Elizabeth's creamy skin flushed, and a smile gently curved her lips. Somebody behind them muttered "Quiet," but Todd didn't care.

As the story unfolded, Todd shifted in his seat again. He'd seen *Casablanca* before but never realized how much of the movie revolved around a love triangle: Ilsa, her husband, and Rick. Elizabeth, Tom, and Todd.

Elizabeth was suddenly stiff in her seat. He noticed a small frown line forming between her brows. *Uh-oh—is Elizabeth realizing the same thing? Is this movie reminding her of Watts too?*

Todd reached over and clasped Elizabeth's hand in his. It felt a little clammy and stiff at first, but Todd gave it a squeeze, and Elizabeth seemed to relax. Still, when she finally turned toward him, her eyes glittered. Todd tensed for a moment, startled. What was making her cry—the movie? Thoughts of Tom Watts? Or even worse—was it something that Todd himself had done?

"Liz," he whispered urgently. "Are—are we moving too fast?"

She smiled, though her eyes were still sad. "How could we be moving too fast?" she asked. "We've known each other forever."

Todd felt a surge of nervous energy charge through him. Letting go of her hand, he reached around, stroking her hair lightly before his hand came to rest on her shoulder. Elizabeth stiffened a bit, and Todd instinctively leaned over to whisper, "Liz, it's OK. It's just me—Todd."

Elizabeth let out a long, slow breath, then leaned her head on Todd's shoulder. Todd rested his cheek on her silken hair as she relaxed completely into his embrace.

*   *   *

I'd forgotten how good Todd smells—so warm and comforting. Elizabeth snuggled into Todd's arm a little closer and rested her head back on his shoulder. Every once in a while Todd's strong hand would lift from her shoulder and trace it lightly with his fingertips. *This is perfect.*

As the movie came to a close, Elizabeth dabbed at her eyes. *Casablanca* always made her cry. Humphrey Bogart's character was tough but loving, strong but tender. *Just like a man's supposed to be,* Elizabeth thought dreamily. *Bogie even made breaking up seem romantic. Rick left Ilsa because he loved her, not because he was trying to hurt her. Unlike certain people.* Elizabeth hastily straightened in her seat.

Tom used to do a killer Bogie impression. Remember, Liz? a voice inside her taunted. A voice that sounded a lot like her own.

Stop, Elizabeth told herself firmly. *You can't think about that. Not now.*

Elizabeth turned her thoughts around by concentrating on *Casablanca*'s beautiful theme music, which still played as the credits rolled. *It's amazing how the true love stories survive over time. This movie is over a half century old, and it still makes me melt. Real love is like that—selfless and beautiful. Real love isn't cruel and mistrustful.*

Against her will, Elizabeth's mind drifted back to a memory she'd wanted desperately to forget. During a stopover on a Caribbean cruise, not long after she and Tom had started dating, she had caught him kissing his ex-girlfriend. A steel band had been playing then, the music swelling as she watched her boyfriend kissing another woman.

"*. . . a kiss is still a kiss. . . .*" The lyrics echoed sadistically in Elizabeth's mind. The band had been playing "As Time Goes By," the signature song from *Casablanca*.

But Elizabeth had given Tom another chance then. She had taken him back. And how had Tom treated Elizabeth in return? After she had confided in him about his father's advances, he hadn't believed her. He hadn't trusted her. He had broken up with her. And on top of it all, Tom didn't seem to regret it one bit.

"What a perfect movie, Liz." Todd wrapped her more tightly in his embrace. He seemed completely oblivious to her sudden change in mood.

Elizabeth tried to hold off the wave of horrible memories that threatened to wash over her. But she couldn't. Tom's heartless words scrolled relentlessly through her mind, accompanied by the image of his cold, cruel smile. He hated her.

Tom Watts hated Elizabeth Wakefield.

The scorching pain rose fast and hard. Elizabeth almost fell over when she shot up out of her seat. The hot sting of tears blurred everything around her.

"Elizabeth, what's wrong?" Todd asked. His voice sounded as if it were coming from the end of a long tunnel.

The small, dark theater had become a tomb. She had to get out before she suffocated. Elizabeth roughly pulled away from Todd's grasping arms and blindly dashed for the aisle. Todd called her name, but it sounded faint and far away. As she ran for the exit her ankle turned once, sending a sharp pain up her leg. She staggered but forced herself to keep moving.

Once safe in the tart night air, she leaned against the side of the theater, gasping and sobbing. A few people passed by and stared, then averted their eyes. Elizabeth felt no shame or embarrassment. All she could feel was the weight of Tom's hatred crushing her.

Just then a warm, strong hand squeezed her shoulder. Elizabeth turned around and gazed up at Todd, his blurred face a picture of loving concern. Letting out another cathartic sob, she fell into his arms. Elizabeth pressed her face against Todd's chest and allowed herself to be soothed by his hand as it stroked her hair. Gradually the tears subsided, and Elizabeth held on to Todd tightly, as if she would never let go.

*　　　*　　　*

I'm totally lost. And now I'm totally late *too,* Jessica fretted. She must have missed her exit back on the freeway because the unpaved country road she had turned down led only to a dead end.

"This is not my fault," Jessica mumbled, staring blankly out the windshield at nothing but a lot of trees, grass, and dirt. *"This is not my fault!"*

Jessica struggled to back up the Jeep so she could turn around. Suddenly her back wheels slid off the road and sank into a marshy ditch. The last straw was now broken. Jessica let out a long, agonized wail.

"It's the Jeep's fault," she reasoned. "Yeah, that's it. The Jeep is conspiring against me today." Jessica pounded the steering wheel with her fist as if to punish the Jeep for bad behavior. Then she bounced up and down in her seat for good measure. Jessica hoped no one could see her pitch a fit, but she knew the only other soul around was a crow that sat perched by the ditch, staring. It cawed derisively and flew off.

"Thanks for nothing," Jessica growled. Gripping the steering wheel, she gunned the engine. After a few torture-filled seconds, the mud finally released the Jeep's back tires. *Wait till Liz sees this,* Jessica thought, catching a glimpse of the mud-spattered back panels. *She's so fussy about keeping the Jeep clean.* Swiftly she completed her U-turn and hit the gas.

Jessica spun out and raced for the main road, tires screeching. At the dead end she had taken just enough time to brush her hair and fix her makeup, but now she was all sweaty and out of sorts. She drove wildly, barely waiting for the lights to change, hurtling around corners. But her neck muscles unclenched when she spotted the sign up ahead. Ridell Road—*finally!* Jessica heaved a huge sigh of relief.

With one hand she dug her miniature atomizer out of her purse and squirted herself generously. Lila had loaned Jessica her most expensive perfume—Moon Dreams—for tonight. *At least I'll* smell *sophisticated,* she reassured herself.

Wow—I had no idea Nick's parents lived in such a nice neighborhood. Jessica drove past well-groomed yards and attractive colonial houses. Her pulse began to slow down, and when she spotted the number 302, she melted with relief. Jessica parked the Jeep carefully by the curb and got out. There it was—the Fox house. Soon Nick would greet her at the door and the whole nightmare would be over.

As Jessica walked up the long driveway she smiled, picturing Nick playing in the yard when he was a little boy. She could just see young Nick leaping around and playing Horse with his friends at the basketball hoop over the garage. *He must have been so adorable,* Jessica thought, imagining his long-lashed green eyes and his thick, tousled hair. He'd probably been a real handful too—just like Jessica herself.

Jessica passed Nick's motorcycle and a silver sedan that was parked close to the garage door. Behind the sedan was a shiny black car.

A Lexus.

Jessica ran to the rear of the Lexus. All her relief and joy slipped away when she saw the car's dented bumper.

And the vanity plate that read Trouble.

Groaning loudly, Jessica spun on her heel. Her just tamed golden hair whipped out behind her as she threw herself into the Jeep, hit the gas, and shot past the Fox house like a lightning bolt. *This can't be real,* she whimpered silently. *This must be the twilight zone.*

Jessica hoped that no one inside the house had spotted her in the driveway—then she'd be home free. But the full realization of what just happened hadn't quite hit her yet.

As she sped down the exit back onto the freeway, it did. *Omigod,* she thought. "Omigod! I crashed into Nick's mother's car! And I screamed at her! Oh, jeez, what a way to make a first impression!"

She headed for the freeway, still shaking and

nervous. "Calm down, girl," Jessica muttered, talking to her reflection in the rearview mirror. "Everything will be just fine. We'll think of something. Stop acting like a basket case." But she couldn't. She *felt* like a basket case—and looked like one too.

Jessica took a long look at the clock on the dashboard. It took her almost a full minute to process the fact that she was supposed to be at the Fox house over an hour and fifteen minutes ago. "I've really blown it this time," Jessica wailed. "I've ruined *everything*. What will Nick think of me now?"

Chapter Six

This must be what being in front of a firing squad is like, Nick thought as he paced the living room, keenly aware of his mother's eyes boring into him. *No, maybe worse.*

"Your girlfriend is over an hour late," she said. "Are you sure she's coming?"

Nick started to answer, but his father stepped in. "Now, Rhoda, maybe the girl got lost. She doesn't live around here, after all. You were a little late yourself."

Mrs. Fox rose majestically from the sofa. "That wasn't my fault. This girl is way beyond being 'a little late.' Nick says she only lives about twenty minutes away, so how on earth could she get lost?"

"Maybe she got stuck in traffic," Nick offered.

"Or maybe she's some kind of a ditz," Mrs. Fox spat out.

"Jessica is *not* a ditz," Nick said evenly, though he was struggling mightily with his temper. "I'm sure she'll be here any minute."

His mother said nothing and glanced significantly at the clock on the wall.

Nick sighed and paced once more around the living room. The entire room was decorated in cool greens and soothing browns. Nick's mother had once explained to him that the colors combined to create an atmosphere of serenity and harmony. But tonight Nick was feeling neither serene nor harmonious.

Jessica, you'd better show up, he begged silently, as though he could mentally persuade her to appear. *After you pushed and pushed for this dinner . . .* He stopped, unable to think of what he would do if she didn't show. A tiny seed of anxiety quickly took root inside him. What if something had happened to her? She was reckless sometimes. Well, *lots* of times. It was one of the many things about Jessica that drove him crazy in both good and bad ways.

"Speaking of flighty girls, you should have seen the one who rammed my car." Mrs. Fox broke the silence, her face flushed with anger. "This rude little thing actually blamed it on me when *she* was the one who wasn't looking where

96

she was going! I've never met such an insolent person in my life. The least she could have done was apologize. But no, this lunatic acted like it was *her* car that was smashed."

Nick caught his father giving him one of his *are-you-thinking-what-I'm-thinking?* looks. *Rammed* was hardly the right word to describe a collision that resulted in such a small dent. He and his father both knew how Mrs. Fox was prone to exaggeration.

"She was a total lunatic," Mrs. Fox went on. "She had the nerve to blame me for the accident!"

"Come on, Mom," Nick blurted, unable to hold back. "You've been in millions of accidents. Face it. You're a crazy driver!"

Mr. Fox nodded. "He's right, you know. You're a loose cannon on the road."

"Well, how do you like that. You're *both* ganging up on me." Mrs. Fox shrugged, belying the wicked twinkle in her eyes. "I admit I may be a little wild, but if you want to see a real spitfire, you should have seen *this* girl—"

The telephone suddenly rang, and Nick slumped in relief. *Jessica!* He rushed to pick it up, saying a quick prayer under his breath.

"Where are you?" he demanded as soon as he heard her voice. He thrust his fingers carelessly through his thick brown hair and shot an uneasy look at his parents. "*Everyone's* been waiting for you."

"I'm so sorry, Nick," Jessica replied in a soft, shaky voice.

Nick was instantly worried. "What happened, Jessica? Are you all right? You didn't get in an accident, did you?"

"N-No," she stammered, sounding extremely un-Jessica-like.

"Then what's the matter?" he barked, bringing the cordless telephone into the foyer for a little privacy.

"Oh, Nick," Jessica whimpered, "I feel just awful. I hate letting you down, but I suddenly got the worst headache! It feels like it could be a migraine or something."

Nick narrowed his eyes suspiciously, his cop's instincts alerted. But why would Jessica lie? She was the one who'd twisted his arm for this dinner. He sighed and struggled to control his mounting irritation. "OK, Jess, I understand. We'll just have to cancel our reservations at the Jambalaya House tonight, but—"

"Wait," she broke in eagerly. "Why don't we do it another night? Wednesday would be perfect! Let's make it the same time, OK?"

"I'll try," he answered gruffly. Nick could practically feel his parents' eyes burning holes into his back. The tension in the room was so thick, he could have spread it on bread and ate it—if he'd had a bizarre liking for severe indigestion.

"I'll call you later," Nick said shortly, and hung up. He wished a magical wind would blow into the house, scoop him up, and carry him at least a hundred miles away. *Oh, well, better face the music,* he thought miserably.

"She's not coming, is she?" his mother demanded. She stood with her hands on her hips, her eyes sharply alert.

Nick slowly, silently counted to ten before opening his mouth. "No, she's not. Jessica is really sorry, but she has a terrible headache. Could we reschedule for Wednesday night?"

His mother nodded. "See? My instincts were right. Ditz City!"

"Mom—"

"Rhoda—" Nick and his father reproached her in unison.

Mrs. Fox dismissed them both with a wave of her well-manicured hand. "Fine, you two can take her side. But Miss Ditz had better show up on Wednesday, or we'll have to cancel this dinner— and any other meeting with this girl—for good!"

All I need is a little peace and quiet. Just some time to sort out my thoughts, Elizabeth decided as she made her way through Dickenson Hall. She was glad the corridors were empty. It was dark, still, and restful—just what Elizabeth needed. She wasn't up to putting on a friendly face for anybody.

Her date with Todd replayed in her mind and kept getting mixed up with the movie they had seen. *"Liz, I think I'm really falling for you . . . again,"* whispered Todd as he walked her home. *"Here's looking at you, kid,"* murmured Humphrey Bogart.

Terrific. She was losing her mind. *That's the last time I see a romantic movie with an ex-boyfriend,* she scolded herself as she turned the key in the lock. *After all, Todd is an ex. Remember, Elizabeth? At least he is . . . for now,* a tiny voice in her head added. She groaned as she opened the door to her room. *Ah, peace.*

"Liz, you're finally home!" cried her sister, who was sprawled on her unmade bed. She was dressed in a stylish pink dress and jacket, but the matching petal pink shoes lay on the floor and her golden hair messily framed her face.

Elizabeth noticed her own cameo necklace hanging from Jessica's neck but was too weary to make an issue of it. Instead she took a deep breath and walked over to put her purse on her desk.

"I can't believe what happened to me tonight. You'll never guess in a million years." Jessica flung an arm over her face.

Elizabeth sighed. "What?"

"Well, sound a little interested, why don't you?" Jessica pouted. "I was on my way to meet Nick and his parents for dinner when this insane woman came to a dead stop at the bottom of the ramp, and—"

"Ramp?" Elizabeth turned to look at her sister, hairbrush in one hand. "What on earth are you talking about, Jessica?"

Her sister shot up from the bed. "If you'd listen to me—," Jessica said indignantly.

"OK, OK." Elizabeth caved in. "Listen, I'm going to make some tea. Want a cup?"

"Tea?" Jessica put her hands on her hips, her blue-green eyes darkening. "How can you think about tea in the middle of my crisis?"

Elizabeth headed over to the microwave. "Mmmm, chamomile tea. Very soothing," she said, waving two tea bags in Jessica's direction.

"OK, make me a cup too," Jessica said quickly. "I could use it after the nightmare I went through tonight. Oh, Liz, it was horrible! There I was, tooling down the freeway, when this new black Lexus stopped dead in front of me at the bottom of a ramp! Before I knew it, I crashed right into it!"

"What!" Elizabeth spun around. "Oh no, don't tell me you wrecked the Jeep."

Jessica glared at her and tapped her foot. "Give me some credit, will you? I noticed this car just sitting there at the bottom of the ramp and slowed down in *plenty* of time. It wasn't even a *real* crash—just a tiny one."

"How tiny?"

Jessica shrugged. "Our Jeep doesn't even have a scratch, but the other car . . ."

"The other car," Elizabeth prompted, feeling resignation wash over her face.

"Has a *teeny* ding in the back. It's so small, you can barely see it."

The microwave beeped. Elizabeth opened it and set the cups of steaming water on the counter. "Right," she said dryly, putting in the tea bags.

"But that's not the worst part," Jessica wailed. "The worst part is that the driver was Nick's mother!"

"Oh, Jess!" Elizabeth gasped. "What happened when she found out who *you* were?"

"She doesn't know," Jessica said with a deep sigh. "Not yet anyway."

Elizabeth couldn't help laughing as she handed her sister her tea. "How did you manage that, Jess? Don't tell me you drove away and left her there."

"*No.* Puh-leeze, Liz," Jessica whined, taking her cup back to her bed. "I stopped and gave her my phone number. For, you know, insurance purposes."

"Great. There go our premiums."

"I *didn't* give her my name," Jessica said through her teeth. "But when I drove up— *late*—to the Fox house, I saw the same Lexus in the driveway, dent and all."

Elizabeth's eyes widened. "What did you do?"

"I got the heck out of there," Jessica answered. "Wouldn't you?"

Elizabeth nodded.

"Then I had to make up an excuse to Nick. I told him I had a humongous headache and asked him to reschedule."

"But that means—"

"Exactly!" Jessica hid her face in her hands. "Wednesday is doomsday! I'll *have* to meet Nick's parents, and when his mother recognizes me, everyone will hate me!"

"Wait a minute." Elizabeth set her cup down on her desk authoritatively. "There has to be a way out of this mess."

"How?" Jessica peered at Elizabeth through her fingers.

"Look, why not send her flowers or candy? You can include a nice little note, apologizing and explaining everything. I'm sure that when Mrs. Fox sees how sincerely sorry you are, she'll understand."

"Do you think that'll really work?"

"Why not?" Elizabeth tapped her finger on her chin. "If you're really polite and honest, I'm sure you'll win her over."

"Liz, you're a genius!" Jessica leaped across the room to hug Elizabeth, nearly spilling two cups of tea in the process. "Thanks a million. You're a lifesaver."

"Don't worry, Jess. Everything'll be just fine."

"I hope so. But for now, I deserve a long, hot shower!" Jessica got changed into her bathrobe in record time, grabbed her shower basket, and darted out the door.

Elizabeth took the two teacups back to the kitchen. She dumped the tea in the sink, watching it swirl down the drain. Elizabeth felt as if her peace of mind was washing away with it. *Some genius and lifesaver,* she thought scornfully. What business did she have giving out advice? She couldn't even straighten out her own love life.

Elizabeth sat down at the table and leaned her chin on her hands. *What am I going to do about Todd?* She sighed deeply. *If only I could solve my own problems as easily as I solved Jessica's.*

"He's still standing up—that means he needs more beer!" someone shouted.

"Chug! Chug! Chug!" the deep-voiced chant began.

"Go for it, Tommy," a lone female voice shrieked, followed by a chorus of drunken squeals.

The Delta Chi frat house was literally rocking and shaking. The stereo was cranked up to an earsplitting volume as the walls strained to hold the seething crowd. With all the bellowing chants, wild laughter, and pounding music, Delta Chi could have broken the sound barrier.

Tom Watts tilted back his head and guzzled down another jumbo-size cup of foamy frat beer. The world swam around him; his head felt as though it was filled with helium. Dozens of grinning faces spun by in a mad blur. Tom closed his eyes and gulped the beer in his other hand even faster. Most of it slid down his throat, but some splattered down his face and shirt. Several empty cups lay crumpled at his feet.

He looked down at the beer dripping from his chin. Wiping his face carelessly on his sleeve, he gulped down the last swallow and flung both empty cups to the ground.

Dack Sanchez and Brett Ryder, both football players, whistled and hooted in approval. Dack raised one of Tom's arms over his head and shouted, "The winner and still champion—Tom Watts!" to a burst of applause and stamping feet.

The air was thick with stale cigarette smoke, strong perfume, and the aroma of spilled beer. For a second Tom's stomach felt quivery, but then he shook himself steady. *This is where the action is,* he said to himself. *This is where I belong. Man, it feels good to be back.*

A pounding rock anthem suddenly blasted through the room. Tom almost lost his balance when a petite redhead pushed her way through the crowd and threw her arms around his neck. "I'm gonna rock your world," she purred in Tom's ear.

Tom barely heard her. His old football buddies swarmed around him, watching with eager eyes. *My friends,* Tom thought dizzily. *These are my friends—these great guys, who'd never let me down. No way; these dudes would never try to spoil my fun.* He let out a wild yodel and lifted the pretty redhead off her feet, spinning her around and shouting, "Par-taaaay!" With the girl still in his arms he careened around the room, crashing into furniture and people like a drunken Frankenstein monster.

His buddies laughed and cheered, chanting, "Go, Wildman! Go, Wildman! Go, Wildman!" as Tom stomped and staggered in an uncoordinated circle.

Tom let out a hearty yell as he dropped the girl clumsily into a chair, which unfortunately happened to be occupied already. The redhead screamed, and the couple she landed on cursed in outrage. Tom simply shrugged it off, his grin so wide he thought his face was stretching.

"Sorry." He snickered unrepentantly. "But tonight I'm in the mood for a brunette!"

E. J. Calhoun, a linebacker, threw his arm around Tom's shoulders and bellowed, "Bring this man a dark-haired beauty! We want women—*now!*"

Calhoun beat a nearby table like a drum, spilling dozens of cups of beer. Nobody noticed the mess.

A willowy girl with long raven hair ran up to Tom and wrapped her arms around his waist. "Here I am—just what the Wildman ordered," she breathed.

Tom grabbed on to the brunette and they began to sway in place, pasted up against each other. The tune was a fast one, but Tom and the girl were oblivious. Was the room actually revolving? Tom clung to the girl and draped himself over her shoulder, letting the spinning room do the dancing for him.

Someone tapped him on the shoulder. A familiar face suddenly appeared, and it frowned with disapproval. Tom released the brunette without a word or a glance.

"Danny, my man!" Tom cried with another face-stretching smile. He stumbled and caught himself. "You're looking pretty ticked, bud, and I think I know why. . . ."

"Why," Danny demanded flatly, not budging an inch when Tom reeled and grabbed on to his shoulder for support.

"Because you're standing there empty-handed!" Tom turned and yelled over his shoulder, "Hey, guys, my bud here needs a brewski!"

"I don't want one, Tom," Danny said, gritting his teeth. "Listen . . ."

Danny's words bounced off Tom's ears and ricocheted around the room while Tom waved at the keg keeper. Instantly someone brought him a fresh cup of beer. It foamed over as Tom thrust it under Danny's nose. "Here ya go, pal. Drink up. Looks like you need it."

Danny sighed and grabbed the cup. "Not now, Tom. I need to talk to you."

"Make it quick." Tom let out a loud belch.

"I know you want to have a good time, but look at yourself, Watts! You can hardly stand up. And you smell like a brewery. You're making me real nervous, buddy."

Tom's smile faded. It was bad enough that Danny wouldn't drink the beer Tom got for him, but now he was acting like the Grim Reaper of frat parties. How could Danny turn on Tom like that?

"Get it in your head, Tom," Danny said urgently. "You've been through this whole scene before. You can't go backward. Getting wasted is not the key to having fun."

Tom laughed. His roommate sounded like a public service announcement. "Wyatt, buddy, you really need to loosen up. Now where'd that beer go? Did you finish it already?" Tom began searching for Danny's beer.

"Tom, listen to me. This is serious." Danny grabbed Tom's shoulders. "I know you're ticked off over what happened today on the quad. But getting messed up like this won't make it go away. You've got to stop before you hurt yourself—or someone else."

Tom would have punched Danny Wyatt right in the nose, but his arm felt too heavy and rubbery. *I don't need a lecture*, he thought. *I don't need someone bringing me down. What I need is another beer.*

"C'mon, Tombo," Danny pleaded. "It's time to go home."

"Mind your own business, Wyatt," Tom snarled, staggering away. "If you're not here to have a good time, then get lost."

"You need help," Danny shouted.

"No, man, *you* need help." Tom turned toward his football buddies. "Hey, guys, I'm feelin' thirsty! Bust open another keg!"

"Whooo!" Calhoun pumped his fist in the air. "All right, Wildman! Chug-a-lug contest!"

Suddenly everyone in the frat house seemed to converge on Tom, chanting, "Wild-*man!* Wild-*man!* Wild-*man!*"

I'm back, Tom thought, turning to the crowd. "I'm back!" he shouted. "Wildman Watts is back!"

Chapter
Seven

Mrs. Fox will adore _me when she sees this,_ Jessica thought. She had been strolling through Sunshine Gifts when she was stopped in her tracks by a foot-high pink-and-white stuffed teddy bear that was sitting alone on the sale table. Jessica couldn't believe her good fortune. Since it was only Monday afternoon, she had plenty of time to deliver the bear and a card before Wednesday evening.

Jessica smiled proudly as she looked at the bear's sugary-sweet face. In its paws was a heart-shaped sign that read I'm beary, beary sorry. "You're too cute," she said out loud. "Mrs. Fox is going to eat you up."

Jessica turned to search for the perfect card to go with her gift. She finally pounced on one with a little dachshund on the front. _Don't put me in the_ *doghouse,* it read. Jessica opened the card. *I had a ruff, ruff day!*

Jessica let out a huge sigh of relief. Sure, the gift and the card were a little corny, but they'd erase any memory Mrs. Fox might have of Jessica's screaming banshee impression on the freeway ramp. Plus it was a proven fact that moms were suckers for this kind of stuff anyway.

"Excuse me," Jessica said to the cashier, "but do you handle gift deliveries here? I *have* to get these to someone by Wednesday afternoon. It's a matter of life and death."

The cashier raised an eyebrow, then smiled. "We sure do. Just fill out the address on this sheet, and we'll take care of the rest."

Wow! Everything's going my way today, Jessica thought with glee as she printed Mrs. Fox's address on the sheet. Then she filled out the card as the cashier began ringing up the gifts. *I'm so sorry I couldn't make it to dinner on Saturday,* she wrote. *I had a terrible headache, and I wanted to meet you at my best. I can't wait to see you on Wednesday! Love, Jessica.*

"Would you like gift wrap with that?" the cashier asked.

"Oooh, yes, please," Jessica replied, sealing the envelope. "The best you have."

"Cash or charge?" The cashier gestured to the total on the register.

Jessica winced. With the price of gift wrap and delivery added in, the total was nearly three times as much as the card and the discounted teddy bear would have been alone. "Um, is a check OK?"

Jessica grumbled as she got out her checkbook. She knew it would be a lot cheaper to just wrap and deliver the gift herself, but she couldn't spare any expense where Nick was concerned. Besides, there was probably no way she could get near the Foxes' house without being discovered.

The main thing is that I'm making brownie points with Mrs. Fox, Jessica reassured herself. *She'll be bowled over when she gets my present and card. I'm sure I'll make an unforgettable impression.*

Todd sat down on his bed and waited. His heart hammered, and his palms were slick. His dorm room seemed suddenly small, as if the walls were closing in on him. He knew Elizabeth didn't have classes yet on Monday. She had to be in her room . . . he hoped.

"Hello?"

Todd's heart spring-vaulted to his throat at the sound of Elizabeth's voice. For a second he couldn't speak.

"Hello? Is anyone there?"

Todd cleared his throat. "It's me, Liz," he croaked, running trembling fingers through his thick hair.

"Oh," she said. "Hi, Todd."

She sure doesn't sound too happy to hear my voice, Todd thought tensely. He decided to rush on with his question before he lost his nerve completely. "Look, Liz, I was just thinking. Um, I was really glad we could get together on Saturday night, and I was wondering . . . how you felt about it?"

"I thought . . ." Elizabeth trailed off and paused for what seemed like an eternity. "It was really nice."

The word *nice* made Todd's heart plummet. *Nice is the kiss of death,* he taunted himself. *Nice is the kind of time you have with your* grandmother.

"I'm glad," Todd replied, "but I felt like something . . . *special* was happening between us. Didn't you?"

There was a silence at the other end of the phone.

"Liz, I'm starting to think that you and I—"

"Hold it." Elizabeth sounded irritated. "I'm sorry, but it's really hard for me to talk about this right now. It's a little sudden, and I don't know what to say."

"Just tell me how you feel, Liz. Please. I have to know."

For a few long moments all Todd heard was the incessant pounding in his temples and the sound of Elizabeth sighing heavily.

"I hope you don't take this the wrong way," Elizabeth began. "I don't want to hurt you. I really don't. So . . . I think it would be best for both of us if we just stay friends."

"But—"

"Please listen, Todd." Elizabeth's voice trembled. "Our relationship is so solid now. It took us a long time to rebuild it. I'm afraid we'll mess things up again if—"

"I would never do anything to hurt you again, Elizabeth," he interrupted, unable to stop himself. "I've made that promise to you. And I'm keeping it."

"I know. I believe you." Elizabeth sniffed. "This is nothing against you. I just can't get involved with anyone right now. I think you know why."

When it came to anything regarding Tom Watts, Todd knew he was powerless to change Elizabeth's mind. She'd made that clear enough to him.

"OK, Liz. I understand." It killed Todd to have to say those words. "We'll cool things down, if that's what you really want."

"Y-Yes, I do," Elizabeth said timidly.

"OK." Todd felt a burning sensation come to his eyes.

"I hope you're not angry with me."

"Of course not, Liz. I have to admit I'm a little disappointed, but I'd never be angry with you. Never."

There was a moment of silence. "Thanks, Todd," Elizabeth said quietly. "Thanks for understanding." There was a click, and then a dial tone.

Todd shook his head as hot tears began to fall from his eyes. He put on his practice sneakers and grabbed his basketball and keys. *I know you're hurting, Elizabeth,* he continued silently as he walked out into the hallway. *And I want to help you forget the pain. But how can I when you won't let go of it?*

"Hi, this is Todd. I'm not here. You know the drill." *Beep.*

Gin-Yung stared at the phone receiver before hanging it up. *Todd even sounds preoccupied on his answering machine,* she thought, chewing her lip. *Still, I should have left a message. I always hate hang-ups.* She picked the receiver back up and pressed redial, crossing her fingers this time. But the machine clicked on again.

"Uh, hi," Gin-Yung said, annoyed at herself

for sounding aimless. "It's only me. I—uh—there's no message. Just called to say hi." Swiftly she hung up.

"Wow, did I sound dumb," Gin-Yung murmured. Outside the window a flock of pigeons fluttered upward against the wet, darkening sky. Gin-Yung got up and pressed her face against the glass pane. She caught a glimpse of the British Museum, one of her favorite places. Nearby was Russell Square, where happy-looking couples strolled hand in hand. Gin-Yung looked away and sighed.

It was hard to believe that not long ago she and Todd had been a happy couple. Todd was an avid ballplayer, and Gin-Yung was just as avid a sports reporter. They had a lot in common—or so she thought.

I should have known when we met on the Homecoming Queen *that there'd be rough seas ahead.* Her weak pun brought a tiny smile to her lips. She and Todd had first gotten to know each other on a college cruise. Todd had literally run right into her, stepping on her foot. But even after that bumpy meeting, it hadn't taken long for them to become a couple. The cruise had been pretty romantic except for a brief, miserable period when Todd had run back to his ex, Elizabeth Wakefield. He'd only been offering her comfort because she had been fighting with her boyfriend, Tom Watts. Still, it had hurt to watch the two of them together.

Gin-Yung shut her eyes and rubbed her temples. *Enough,* she thought. All this moping and moaning wasn't like her. She was tough. She could handle anything.

Jamie Lynn Tiller, Gin-Yung's roommate, looked up from her book. "Did you get Todd's answering machine again? I just hate those things. I always hang up the instant I get one on the line."

Gin-Yung methodically smoothed down her khaki skirt, tucked in her oxford shirt, and reached in her backpack for her notepad. "I guess Todd's out for the evening," she said with a forced casual tone.

Jamie Lynn was from southeast Texas and dreamed of being a professional cheerleader coach. Journalism was her minor, and Jamie had signed up for the London Sports Journalism Program to broaden her education. But for Gin-Yung the London internship was the opportunity of a lifetime. Soccer, or football, as it was called in Europe, was the hottest sport around, and Gin-Yung was a natural to report on it.

Even though their backgrounds were totally different, Gin-Yung and Jamie Lynn had become fast friends. But even Jamie Lynn's good cheer couldn't keep Gin-Yung's spirits up lately.

Gin-Yung bent over her notepad and began jotting down story ideas, but her mind couldn't stop wandering. *I miss California. I miss the sunshine, rainless days, and the ocean. Most of all I miss Todd.*

Jamie Lynn apparently wasn't fooled. "You're not worrying, are you, Gin-Yung? Why, Todd seems like the devoted type, even though the two of you decided to go 'nonexclusive' this year."

"Maybe that wasn't such a great idea." Gin-Yung suddenly felt exhausted, every limb aching as if weighed down with bricks. It even hurt to hold her pen. She dropped everything and stretched out on her bed, eyes closed. All she wanted to do was sleep—for about a thousand hours!

"You're not thinking he's out with another girl, are you?"

Gin-Yung opened her eyes and studied Jamie Lynn's honey blond hair, feeling an anxious chill creep up her spine. *That same blond hair . . . no, don't be silly,* she told herself. *Elizabeth Wakefield is deeply in love with Tom Watts now. They're the ultimate power couple.*

"Todd sounded so funny the last time we talked," Gin-Yung replied after a long pause. "I guess I *am* worrying."

Jamie Lynn frowned. "Well, I think you should put those thoughts right out of your head. Todd's probably just at class or practice or something. You forget there's a time difference between here and California."

"Yeah, you're right," Gin-Yung said with a yawn.

"Besides, he probably sounded funny because he was stressing out over an exam. Face it, Gin-Yung, long-distance relationships are always a little weird. I guess I'm glad that I didn't leave a boyfriend back in Texas."

Gin-Yung remained silent as her jaw tightened painfully.

"Are you feeling all right, Gin-Yung?"

"I'm fine," she answered quickly, feeling weak tears gather in her eyelashes. She forced herself to pick up her notebook again.

Jamie Lynn got up and headed for the door. "I'm going over to Avalon's for some zucchini and nut pies. I can't stand the thought of eating another meal at the cafeteria. If I have to face one more plate of lamb pasties, I'll curl up and die." Jamie Lynn wrinkled her nose and grimaced.

Gin-Yung smiled, beating back the tears with her lashes.

"Why don't you come with me?" Jamie Lynn asked.

Gin-Yung shook her head. "The last thing I need right now is food."

"Are you sure?" Jamie Lynn persisted.

Gin-Yung nodded emphatically.

Jamie Lynn knitted her brows. "What if I

bring you back some food? You know Avalon makes the best veggie muffins around. You're looking skinny, Gin-Yung. You need to eat."

Gin-Yung groaned. "OK, you convinced me." Gin-Yung would have said anything to get her roommate to leave. She liked Jamie Lynn a lot, but she ached for some private time.

Once Jamie Lynn was gone, Gin-Yung finally let her tears fall freely. *Please don't forget me, Todd,* her heart called out. *I need you now, more than ever.*

Chapter Eight

Elizabeth couldn't find Henry the Eighth. After her fifth try she burst into tears. The pages of her textbook swam in front of her. Her Tuesday afternoon world history class was only a few hours away, and preparing for it seemed like an impossible task.

Choking back a sob, Elizabeth got up to reheat her cup of coffee in the microwave. She'd been sifting through the seven-hundred-page book for over twenty minutes and still hadn't tracked down the right section. The index was all wrong, full of typos or something.

Even so, she already knew plenty about the infamous king of England. Old Henry had gone through his six wives like tissues—some he'd had killed, and some had died on their own. All of those women, either beheaded or dead by some other tragic means . . .

Elizabeth laid her head down on her arms and sobbed even harder. Her head ached, and her eyes burned. *I just can't take the uncertainty in my life! At least old Henry knew what he wanted—as many women as possible.* Tears fell down into her textbook and rolled toward the center, where the pages met.

I don't know anything, except that right now I need someone to comfort me, she thought desperately. *I need Todd.*

"Jeez, Liz. I know studying is a bore, but I'd never let it drive me to tears."

Elizabeth lifted her head and blinked. Her sister was standing before her in short denim cutoffs and a tangerine halter top. She seemed to be watching Elizabeth carefully.

"It's not st-studying that's making me cry," Elizabeth stammered, wiping her eyes with the back of her hand.

"Then what is it?"

Elizabeth sighed. "It's Todd, Jess. I talked to him on the phone yesterday and told him I didn't think we should go out. I said we should just be friends."

Jessica pulled up a chair and sat down. "Is that a good thing or a bad thing? I mean, I thought you were long over old Todd."

"I thought I was too. But now I'm not sure. Maybe I made a mistake by telling him that. A big mistake."

"Well, Liz, you're entitled to change your mind. You know how they say it's the woman's prerogative and all that."

Elizabeth crinkled her nose. "That sounds so sexist, Jess."

"All the same, if you're falling for Todd again, you should tell him." Jessica paused and squinted dramatically. "*Are* you falling for him again?"

"I'm not sure." Elizabeth moaned. "That's the problem. How can I even think of Todd when I just broke up with Tom? I'm not the type to jump from guy to guy."

"Unlike me, you mean," Jessica said dryly.

"No! I didn't—"

Jessica waved a hand. "Never mind, I'm not offended. But let's get real here, Liz. What does time have to do with anything? If you want Todd, then go for it!"

"But—"

"No buts about it. Follow your instincts. Go for the gusto!"

"You sound like a beer commercial," Elizabeth said with a reluctant giggle.

Jessica shrugged. "Who cares? You love Todd, don't you?"

Elizabeth lowered her gaze and smoothed a crease in her jeans. "Yes," she whispered. "I do."

"You want to go out with him, right?"

Jessica demanded, leaning forward in her seat.

Elizabeth nodded. "Yeah, you're right. I do want to see Todd."

"Is there a snowball's chance that you and Tom will get back together?"

Elizabeth shook her head, fighting back the threat of tears. "No. There's none."

Her sister broke into a big grin. "Well, Liz, there's your answer. Who knows? Todd may be the right man for you after all. I used think he was kind of a bore, but he's turned into a real MBOC."

"What, may I ask, is an MBOC?" Elizabeth asked, slightly bemused.

"Major Babe on Campus," Jessica retorted. "Now, as much as I'd absolutely love to spend the whole day hashing out the details of your love life, I promised Lila we would study together." Jessica dramatically picked up her bag and headed out the door with a flourish.

Elizabeth sat stunned. Since when did Jessica Wakefield become a relationship counselor? She made finding true love sound so uncomplicated, as if Elizabeth could just erase Tom from her mind and leap into Todd's arms.

If only it really was that easy, Elizabeth thought as she walked over to the phone. With a shaky finger she dialed Todd's number. *It's at times like this when I'd do anything to live Jessica's life. It's so much simpler!*

*   *   *

Todd's strong arm firmly encircled Elizabeth's shoulders, and every so often his lips brushed her hair. Her head fit perfectly in the crook of his neck. The sun warmed her bare shoulders, and a gentle breeze caressed her skin. She felt so wonderful, she thought she might be dreaming.

But Elizabeth was awake, and everything around her was real—including Todd. When she had called him late that morning, she had been nervous about admitting to him that she'd changed her mind. After all, almost a whole day had passed since she'd told Todd they shouldn't be more than friends. Even now the memory made her blush a little.

But Todd had been accepting and understanding—he wasn't the kind of guy to say, "I told you so." And when Todd had asked if she wanted to go to a concert later that afternoon at the Sweet Valley Bandshell, Elizabeth accepted eagerly. She loved live music, especially outdoor concerts. And she wanted more than anything to be with Todd again.

When Todd picked her up at Dickenson Hall, he had looked incredibly handsome in a maroon polo shirt and chinos, his hair sleek from a recent shower. And even now, as they sat together on a blanket in the late afternoon sun,

Elizabeth couldn't help thinking, *Jessica is right. Todd* is *an MBOC.*

As the Mango Seeds filled the air with vibrant music, Elizabeth scanned the grounds, amazed at how many couples were at the concert. A man and woman sitting directly in front of her had been holding hands and gazing into each other's eyes ever since she and Todd got there. *I wonder if Todd and I look like that?* Elizabeth asked herself. *Sometimes it's easy to tell when two people belong together.*

"I'm so happy you wanted to do this, Liz," Todd murmured in her ear. "The weather's great, and so's the music. But most of all I'm just happy to be here with you." He kissed her temple gently.

Elizabeth responded by wrapping her arms tightly around Todd's waist. "I'm happy too, Todd. I really am," she replied, turning to look up at him. Elizabeth felt her face heat up as Todd's warm brown eyes locked onto hers.

Todd is so intense, Elizabeth thought nervously. *More so now than ever before.* Suddenly they were interrupted by applause and cheers. The Mango Seeds had just finished their set, and Elizabeth felt almost relieved when Todd took his arm away to clap enthusiastically. *What's wrong with me?* Elizabeth wondered as she clapped too. *There's nothing for me to be afraid of. Nothing.*

As the noise died down Todd checked the flyer he kept in his pocket. "The next band is Fever on Ice. They have a new CD coming out."

Elizabeth stretched out her legs and exhaled. "Oh, right—I've heard of them. They're supposed to be really good." Elizabeth didn't admit to Todd that she had only heard of them because WSVU had been publicizing the concert for weeks.

As Fever on Ice began to set up, Todd got to his feet. "How about a hot dog or some nachos?" he asked, a hungry glint in his eye. "Or some chicken wings, or how about a hamburger? Or some popcorn?"

"Why not get one of everything?"

"Don't kid me. You know I just might."

Elizabeth laughed. "Well, I could go for a hot dog. You, however, look like you could eat a truckload."

Todd nodded. "I'm starving."

"And a carrot-garlic-oat shake won't do the trick, I guess."

"Not in this lifetime." He bent down to give her a quick kiss on the forehead. "I'll be right back. Don't go anywhere."

"I won't." Elizabeth wrapped her arms around her knees as she watched Todd stride across the grounds toward the impossibly long line at the concession stand. Then she turned to the stage.

Fever on Ice's lead singer was a pretty young African American woman whose long hair draped around her like a mantle. Her brightly colored dashiki complemented her full-bodied voice. Each song she sang was better than the last.

Elizabeth swayed to the music. It was almost as good as the last time she was here. Of course, this was nothing like classical. . . .

Suddenly Elizabeth shivered. Goose bumps broke out on her skin. *Why do I have to remember that night now? Mr. Conroy may have spoiled that concert, but I can't let him ruin this one.*

The orchestra had performed Beethoven, and the chorus had just begun singing "Ode to Joy" when . . .

Stop it right now, Elizabeth told herself.

But Elizabeth couldn't stem the flow of her horrible memories. *How could George Conroy make a move on me with Tom sitting right there? Rubbing against my arm once might have been an accident, but then when he did it again . . .* Just thinking about it made her flesh crawl.

"Hey, beautiful, I bet you're hungry."

Elizabeth looked up, relieved to see Todd standing above her, his arms full of food and a drink in each hand. He handed her a hot dog with everything and a soda, then sat down with a broad grin. Elizabeth wasn't really in the mood to eat, but she was glad

130

for the excuse to put her chilling memories aside.

Fever on Ice started a new ballad with a haunting riff as Elizabeth took a bite of her hot dog. She felt a little mustard smear along the side of her mouth. Without a moment's hesitation Todd reached over and wiped it away gently.

Elizabeth could feel herself blushing as she put down her hot dog. "Thanks."

"Welcome," Todd replied. He gestured toward the stage. "They're really good, don't you think? Not too country, not too bluesy—just a little of both. And they're not too retro or too cutting edge either."

"They have just the right mix of the old and the new." Elizabeth's eyes locked with Todd's as she wrapped her arms around his neck. Todd's head leaned in to meet hers. "Just like you and me," she murmured, just before their lips touched.

"*Grrowl!* I'm hungrier than King Kong!" Tom shouted, thumping his chest as he entered the Conroy home. "I could eat a whole tree. Or make that a whole forest."

Mary and Jake erupted with giggles. "Are you really gonna eat a tree?" Jake asked innocently.

"Don't be silly." Mary tossed back her long blond hair. "He's just teasing."

George Conroy came up behind the kids.

"All jokes aside, we've got a big dinner planned. I don't think you'll leave here hungry, Tom."

Tom smiled warmly at his father. Knowing Mr. Conroy, he was in for a feast. "Need any help setting the table?"

"Hannah's got everything under control," Mr. Conroy announced heartily. "All you'll need is a good appetite."

"I've got that covered." Tom sank back into the cloud-soft couch. Hannah was the family cook and a genius in the kitchen. The house was filled with the tantalizing aroma of prime rib and apple pie. Tom's stomach growled in anticipation.

Jake darted across the living room and landed next to Tom on the couch. "Let's play Monopoly," he begged, bouncing up and down.

"Dad, Jake's being bossy again," Mary whined. She turned to her little brother. "We don't want to play another stupid old Monopoly game. I want to tell Tom about my cello lessons."

"You're just jealous 'cause you always lose," Jake retorted. "Besides, nobody cares about the cello."

Mr. Conroy looked up from the bar, where he was pouring Perrier into glasses of ice. "Now, kids, let's not fight. We've got plenty of time for both Monopoly and the cello."

Mary and Jake shot each other equally triumphant looks.

Tom jumped up to help Mr. Conroy carry the glasses over.

"Oh, cool," Jake crowed, holding up his bubbling glass. "I'm drinking champagne."

Mary rolled her eyes upward but didn't say anything. She sipped daintily and demurely crossed her ankles.

Mr. Conroy settled himself into his favorite wing back chair. "You know, if you kids act too wild, you may scare Tom away. He may not want to come back."

The kids' shrieks of protest were quickly squelched by the arrival of Hannah, who smiled and announced that dinner was ready. Tom and the Conroys followed her into the majestic dining room.

What a spread, Tom thought, surveying the table that had been laden with some of his favorite foods. He sat down and hungrily cut into his butter-soft prime rib.

Mary was passing the plate of rolls to Mr. Conroy when Jake grabbed one and put it on top of his head.

"Look at my hat, Tom," he said with a wide, mischievous grin.

Tom pretended to study him seriously. "You look pretty good, Jake. Just like a giant roll!"

"Hey, no, I don't," protested Jake. In the blink of an eye he threw his roll at Tom.

"Now, kids—," Mr. Conroy began.

"You are *such* a creep, Jake," Mary said at the same time.

Tom slid out of his chair and clutched his chest. He closed his eyes and let out a loud moan. "I've been hit! Mortally wounded!"

Jake snickered. Mary peered under the table at Tom, who was lying motionless. He winked at her and slid back into the chair, deftly scooping the roll from the floor.

Tom threw his father an apologetic look. "Sorry, I'm supposed to be a role model, aren't I?"

Before Mr. Conroy could reply, Jake hollered, "You are a role model—a *roll* model! Get it?" Jake laughed so hard, he almost spit out the milk he was drinking.

Mary sighed and shook her head. "Sure, twerp, we get it."

Without missing a beat Jake went on the offensive, and the two began giggling and whispering, soon forgetting about Tom and their father.

Mr. Conroy passed the sauteed green beans to Tom. "The kids just adore you, Tom. You've been a marvelous influence. Ever since their mother died, it's been hard on them. They needed another caring adult in their lives."

"I'm glad you feel that way," Tom answered quickly. "They've made a big difference in my life too."

"I just hope they're not taking up too much of your time." Mr. Conroy put down his fork. "The truth is, I'm worried about you, Tom. I'd like to see you get back in the swing of things. I'd hate to see you spending all your free time here."

Tom shook his head. "Don't worry. I've got a very active social life." *George doesn't need to know* how *active,* he assured himself. "I'm fine. I'm having a great time."

Mr. Conroy hesitated and averted his gaze. "I don't suppose you've spoken to Elizabeth lately. . . ."

The prime rib Tom had just eaten seemed to turn into a blob of cement in his stomach. He gripped his water glass so hard that for a second he thought he cracked it. *Calm down, Watts,* he told himself. "Of course I haven't spoken to Elizabeth." *And after our last meeting I doubt we'll ever talk again,* he added silently.

Tom looked up, realizing Mr. Conroy was waiting for him to continue. "Elizabeth doesn't exist for me. She destroyed any chance of us ever being together. After she—"

Mr. Conroy broke in quickly. "That's all right, son, you don't have to explain." He cleared his throat and paused a moment before continuing. "I was thinking about you playing football again, Tom. Some of my best college memories involve that game. . . ."

From the look on Elizabeth's face the other day, Tom thought as Mr. Conroy rambled on, *I'd think she was sorry about what she did. That is, if I didn't know better.* Tom forced himself on a different train of thought in order to stave off the oncoming wave of agony. *Why should I worry? She has Wilkins to comfort her. Elizabeth is obviously a woman who looks out for her own interests. Even if that means lying and destroying a fine man's reputation.*

Elizabeth really was deceptive and devious. Pretending she cared about Tom, pretending she wanted to reunite him with the Conroys— *All she really ever cared about was herself,* he concluded silently.

Tom suddenly felt a sharp pain in his jaw. He had no idea how hard he was clenching his teeth. The hands in his lap had formed white-knuckled fists. *Never again will I let Elizabeth Wakefield hurt me. She's dead and gone. And soon even the memories of her will be dead too.*

Chapter Nine

"Maybe I'll run off to Siberia," Jessica said morosely, leaning her chin in her hands. Her books were scattered across the table in the student union study lounge. Jessica couldn't remember the last time she'd met Lila on a Tuesday afternoon for a study session. But of course, this was an emergency. In just a day she'd be meeting Nick's parents for dinner.

Lila bounced up and down on the squeaky vinyl cushions of a nearby sofa. "This place is in dire need of an interior designer. SVU *really* needs to do some serious work down here." She brushed her beautifully manicured hand across the scarred surface of an end table and shook her head as if it were a hopeless cause.

"Jeez, Lila, I hate to interrupt your decorating trauma, but we are only talking about my life—my entire future—here." Jessica huffily flipped her hair over her shoulder and glared at her best friend.

Lila sighed. "You're making too big a deal out of this, Jess. You just need to remain calm. That's what I do when Bruce is getting on my nerves. I hold on to my self-control and handle the situation with dignity." A smile of self-satisfaction spread across Lila's face.

Jessica snorted. She had a crystal clear memory of the most recent fiasco involving Lila's so-called self-control—when Lila's equally rich boyfriend, Bruce Patman, had bought a doughnut shop for Lila. The shop had almost gone bankrupt, and Lila had ended up in a screaming match with Bruce. Jessica couldn't keep herself from chuckling at the memory.

Lila's brown eyes flashed. "Fine, Jessica, if you don't think I'm qualified to give you advice—"

"I *do* need your help, Li. Really. This is a total disaster." Jessica covered her face with her hands. "What will I do when Mrs. Fox realizes I'm the one who crashed into her car? Nick will be furious—he'll hate me!"

Lila arranged the folds of her gauzy floral skirt and frowned thoughtfully. "Let's see, you're supposed to meet Nick and his parents tomorrow night, right?"

"Don't remind me," moaned Jessica.

"You sent Mrs. Fox a gift and a card as an apology for missing dinner, right?" Lila flicked off a piece of imaginary lint from her mint green silk blouse.

Lila's Nancy Drew impression is pretty pathetic, Jessica thought, biting her tongue. *But I'm desperate, and Lila's my last hope.*

"Well . . . ?" Lila nudged.

Jessica nodded. "Yeah, I did. Let's just hope a cute stuffed bear does the trick. Of course, once Mrs. Fox figures out it was *me* who dented her car, I'd better plan on sending diamonds, or at least a magnum of Dom Pérignon. I mean, extreme situations demand extreme actions."

Lila straightened her own diamond tennis bracelet. "That would be gauche, Jess. Never send expensive gifts too soon in the relationship."

"There's not even going to *be* a relationship if we don't think of something. And I'm not just talking about Nick's mother. Nick himself may dump me when he finds out the truth." Distractedly Jessica shoved her books to one side, accidentally knocking one off the table. When she bent to pick it up, she blinked in surprise. She'd completely forgotten that she and Lila were supposed to be studying.

"Don't panic," Lila advised. "I feel an idea germinating."

139

"Germinating?" Jessica stared at her. "You have been brushing up on your vocabulary, haven't you? Don't tell me you're turning into an egghead like my sister!"

"Don't be silly," Lila answered absentmindedly. "You know it means 'evolving' or 'sprouting.'"

After a short silence Jessica grew impatient. "Well, Lila, has anything sprouted yet? Or do I have to book a flight to Siberia after all?"

Lila arched a slim brow. "Testy, aren't we? But anyone would be in your situation, I suppose."

Jessica gave her best friend a long, hard scowl.

Lila leaned forward, her eyes sharp and focused. "The main thing is that you don't want Nick's mother to think you're some kind of delinquent or something. I mean, you do have that drug bust on your record already."

"Lila! How can you bring that up at a time like this?" Jessica's face flushed in outrage.

"It may have been a mistake, but it still looks bad, Jessica," Lila warned.

"I know, I know." Jessica's spirits sank even further. *Maybe this really is a no-win situation,* she thought.

"All's not lost, though," Lila said with a growing smile. "All you have to do is call Mrs. Fox and apologize for the accident."

"What? Are you nuts!" Jessica snapped upright in her chair.

"Wait," Lila insisted, holding up a slim hand. "You gave her your phone number but not your name, right?"

Jessica nodded solemnly.

"Then you have nothing to worry about. You call her, but you pretend you're someone else. Let's say you call yourself . . . Margaret. By the time you actually *meet* her, you'll have smoothed her ruffled feathers already. Once she talks to you *in person,* you can be your cute and charming self. She'll instantly forgive you!"

"It *could* work," Jessica murmured as if to herself.

"It will, trust me," Lila asserted.

Jessica gazed off into space and mulled over Lila's plan. Her mood brightened. "You know, Li, that's not a bad idea. Mrs. Fox can shoot her mouth off at Margaret. This way, she can get it out of her system. By the time she sees me, she'll have calmed down. Pretty smooth, Lila."

"I don't know why you're surprised, Jessica," Lila replied with a toss of her head. "I'm the mistress of strategy. I can think my way out of any dilemma."

"Except when it involves doughnuts."

"Hey, I made a profit when I sold that shop to my father, plus I made money for the women's shelter too!" Lila said haughtily.

"I know. I was just kidding," Jessica said

quickly, eager to turn the conversation back around. "I'm grateful, Li, really."

Lila smiled with self-satisfaction. "Think nothing of it. That's what friends are for."

"That settles it. I'll phone Mrs. Fox tomorrow as . . ." Jessica shot Lila a devilish smile.

"Margaret!" they exclaimed simultaneously.

Lila grinned. "Piece of cake."

"Once this is over, I can concentrate on important stuff, like Nick and me." Jessica stretched with relief. This was going to be easy! "I don't know why I was worrying. Your plan is perfect, Lila."

"Like I said, Jess, piece of cake."

"This is wonderful," Elizabeth said dreamily, watching the rain pour down in silvery sheets. The sky was cinder gray and full of low black clouds. But she was indoors, snug and warm, with an adoring, attractive man sitting across from her.

Elizabeth turned away from the window and caught Todd smiling at her. He reached across the booth and took her hand.

"I'm glad you don't have any classes until the afternoon, Liz," Todd said. "After I got home from the concert last night, all I could think about was when we could get together again."

"Me too." Elizabeth blushed and looked down at the smooth Formica table. She was thrilled that Todd had asked her out to lunch at Silly Sam's Diner. It hadn't been open for long, but already Elizabeth had heard great things about it. The decor was modernized, imitation fifties. Brightly colored ceramic tiles decorated the floors, walls, and countertops. The red leather booths were huge and enclosed—perfect for privacy. Lucite lamps shaped like dice hung over each table. The jukebox in the corner played CDs instead of records.

"The waitresses' outfits are pretty wild." Todd pointed out a girl in a flippy miniskirt with a poodle printed on it.

"Well, at least this isn't another Kitty's," Elizabeth deadpanned.

Todd laughed. "I still can't believe you went through with that, Liz."

"It wasn't easy, but it was worth it. It was about time someone blew the whistle on Kitty's. I mean, if a restaurant only hires big-chested women to fill out their skimpy little uniforms, that's completely discriminatory. And the fact that the place was totally sexist sure didn't help their case any."

"That's one thing, Liz. But the fact that you went undercover and actually got a job there— that's amazing. From what I read in your article,

143

the guy who ran Kitty's sounded like a real creep."

Elizabeth shuddered. "He was pretty awful, but I think the big, stupid padded bra I had to wear was even worse. No, wait, the hardest part was dealing with some of the male customers. They treated us waitresses as if we were part of a hands-on display."

"That was a great story, Liz," Todd said genuinely. "I was really proud of you when I read it."

Satisfaction coursed through Elizabeth's veins as she quietly replied, "Thanks."

They were quiet for a while. A Tony Bennett classic drifted through the air, slow and romantic. Elizabeth lost herself in the music.

Todd leaned across the table. "Liz, I wanted to say . . ." He trailed off, his voice soft and slightly hesitant. "I don't want to push you. If you think things are going too fast, please tell me."

"OK," Elizabeth answered quietly, her heart swelling with pride. Was this sensitive, mature guy really Todd Wilkins—the same Todd Wilkins who'd broken up with her so harshly when they first started college? *No, he's not the same guy as he was then,* Elizabeth realized. *He's totally changed—for the better.*

But as they stared deeply into each other's eyes, Elizabeth felt a familiar pang. Todd might be a changed man, but could her feelings for him ever be the same as they used to be? Judging from the feelings of warmth flowing over her and the dizzy sensation in her head, Elizabeth realized it was possible. *This isn't just déjà vu*, Elizabeth decided. *It's much more than that. This is real.*

"Wait right here," Todd said with a mysterious smile. He got up and strolled over to the jukebox. Elizabeth watched him, wondering if Todd was looking for "Yesterday." But she knew that song didn't really belong on a fifties-era jukebox.

But when the new song began, Elizabeth's heart beat a little faster. She recognized it immediately. It was Nat King Cole's "Unforgettable." Todd stood at the jukebox and faced her, his loving look sending her back to a time before she ever knew the meaning of heartbreak. Back when true love seemed totally within reach. Back when Todd mattered more to her than anything.

Todd walked back to the booth and slid into the seat next to her. Their legs grazed under the table. He turned toward her and touched her forehead with his.

"I love this song," Elizabeth began. "It reminds me of . . . a lot of things."

"Me too." Todd tilted Elizabeth's chin upward. His deep eyes held hers for what seemed a blissful eternity. "I've never forgotten you, Liz. I don't think I've ever stopped loving you."

Elizabeth gently raised a fingertip to his lips. "You don't need to say anything, Todd. I know."

Elizabeth closed her eyes as Todd kissed her hand gently. *I wonder why it's taken me so long to realize the truth,* she said silently. *Todd and I belong together.*

Tom dashed through the unexpected downpour, muddy water splashing up onto his khakis. *Who cares?* he thought drearily. *I'm miserable anyway. I might as well be wet* and *miserable.* He didn't have a raincoat or an umbrella, and his car was parked a good six blocks away.

Face it, Watts, he taunted himself. *You can only pretend you're on top of the world when you have an audience. You can't fool yourself when you're alone.* He was shivering and soaking wet. Deep down, Tom didn't care if it kept on raining forever.

As long as he was drinking and partying or hanging out with his new family, Tom was fine. Or at least he could pretend he was on the surface. But this afternoon, as Tom went out to run his errands at the copy shop and the bookstore, intense gloom hit him like a freight train. He had tried to distract himself by thinking about the TV station and the football team, but nothing worked. His misery only deepened.

I've got to pull myself out of this, Tom told himself. *I've been trying to put up a front for days, but beneath it all I've still been miserable. If only there was someone I could talk to.* The rain suddenly intensified and thunder cracked overhead, as if it were a forewarning of the shattering realization Tom was about to make.

I miss Elizabeth, Tom confessed to himself. *I miss her so much, it hurts.*

But there was no one Tom could turn to, no one he could share his confused thoughts with. Tom had made a fool of himself in front of Danny, so that option was closed. It would be impossible to talk to Mr. Conroy about Elizabeth— her accusations of him still made Tom seethe. *If my real dad was alive,* Tom thought sadly, *he would listen.*

The only other person Tom ever allowed himself to confide in was Elizabeth, and the irony shot through him like a red-hot bullet. *I could always pour my feelings out to her. She was my best friend, the person I most trusted.* But that was then.

Tom shifted his packages from arm to arm and jogged across the street. A dump truck lumbered by, splashing him with more dirty water. Tom didn't even flinch. He simply trudged to an empty bench and sat down, letting the downpour hit him with full force.

Tom slouched down on the bench, staring blankly at the brightly lit diner across the street—he couldn't make out the name. The heavy needles of rain obscured the sign. Tom realized then that he hadn't eaten lunch, but he wasn't all that hungry; his stomach felt leaden. *I could go in and get a cup of coffee, but why bother? Coffee's not going to help.*

The sky darkened further as a cloud burst overhead, sending even more rain down in powerful, slashing sheets. Tom didn't make an effort to move from the bench. He had resigned himself to being soaked—and depressed—to the skin.

Wildman Watts had evaporated. The rain washed him away.

No more lying to yourself, Watts. Tom sank even lower on the bench and dropped his chin to his chest. *You've hit rock bottom. You can't get any lower than this.*

"So the dog turned to the mother cat and said, 'Sorry! I didn't mean to hurt your *felines*.'"

Elizabeth shook her head and laughed. "You've told me a lot of bad jokes over the years, Todd, but that has to be one of your worst."

"Thanks, Liz," Todd said, finishing up the last of his burger. "Don't try to hurt *my* 'felines' or anything."

"Cute, Todd," Elizabeth said, relaxing into her side of the booth. When their food had finally arrived, the plates had been so huge that Todd had to move back to his own side in order for them to actually eat.

Elizabeth realized, with a twinge of guilt, that she had been slightly grateful for the interruption. The intensity between the two of them had made her feel as though she needed some breathing room. Even so, she hadn't asked Todd if they could slow things down.

The meal had been delicious, and Todd had put her completely at ease with his funny stories and jokes. She was in no hurry to leave, and it had nothing to do with the downpour outside.

Elizabeth gazed dreamily out the window. It looked as if the rain was starting to let up a bit. Suddenly the smile on her face evaporated.

It can't be! Elizabeth stared harder and wiped the condensation from the glass. *It just can't be him. Why here? Why now?*

Tom Watts was sitting on a bench across the street, looking wetter and more miserable than the scroungiest stray cat. His worn expression and stooped shoulders made Elizabeth catch her breath. Even in his darkest moments, Elizabeth had never seen Tom look so bleak.

He misses me, she sensed intuitively. *I didn't believe it—didn't want to believe it until just now. But he misses me as much as I—*

As I miss him.

Everything around Elizabeth began to blur and tremble. *I can't lie to myself,* she admitted silently. *I still love him, but . . .*

Elizabeth fought to hold back the feelings she had worked so hard to suppress. Could she ever forgive Tom for not trusting her—the woman he had supposedly loved and believed in? Could she ever forget the horrible words he'd spit at her? The truth was, she couldn't forgive *or* forget. Tom had betrayed her completely.

But look at him, she argued silently. *Look how lonely and vulnerable he is. . . .*

"Liz!" Todd's voice made her jump.

Elizabeth caught a glimpse of her reflection in the window. Her face was stark white. She looked down briefly at her shaking hands, then turned guiltily to Todd. He was staring out the window, his face hard.

"I was going to ask you what was wrong," he began deliberately, "but I guess I can see that for myself."

"I'm sorry, Todd." Elizabeth had to force her voice past the lump in her throat. "I don't . . . I don't know what to say."

"Why don't you tell me how you feel. How you *really* feel." Todd looked as shell-shocked as Elizabeth felt.

Elizabeth's eyes brimmed with unshed tears, and she fought to blink them back. "Oh, Todd . . . please don't ask me to explain." A lone tear slid to the end of her long lashes. "I really thought I was over him. But . . . I'm just so confused."

"Maybe you do need more time." Todd's voice was solemn.

"Maybe."

Todd shifted in his seat and locked his eyes onto Elizabeth's. "I know you're upset, Liz, but don't forget what he did to you. Watts doesn't deserve you. Remember, he called you a liar—and worse."

"*Don't* remind me."

Todd looked down at the table. "I'm sorry. I was out of line."

Elizabeth struggled to find the right words. "I wish I could turn off my feelings, Todd. I hate being torn like this. But I can't help the way I feel. I'm sorry."

Todd didn't respond. His eyes remained fixed on the table.

"That's all I can say. I'm sorry."

Todd looked up at her, impatiently shoving his milk shake to one side. "I don't want to tell you what to do, Elizabeth, but don't you think it's time you got on with your life?"

Elizabeth took a deep breath, unable to answer.

"Don't let Watts mess with your head. Let yourself be happy for once." Todd's deep brown eyes revealed a combination of deep caring and slight bitterness. Elizabeth broke contact and looked down, focusing on a crack in the salt-shaker.

"*Please,* Liz," Todd pleaded. "I'm not even talking about myself here. I'm talking about *you.* Do yourself a favor and move on."

"I c-can't," Elizabeth choked out as she began to let the tears fall. "Please don't think I led you on, Todd. I didn't mean to do that."

Slowly Todd reached across the table and placed a finger under Elizabeth's chin, turning her face up to meet his. The corners of his mouth were tight, his eyebrows pinched.

Elizabeth's lips trembled. "Honestly, Todd, I thought I was ready."

"OK, Liz. I can't tell you how to feel. I just wish . . ." He trailed off and stroked Elizabeth's chin briefly. Todd paused a moment before he stood, picked up the bill, and threw a few dollars onto the table for a tip. "Promise me one thing," he began.

Elizabeth nodded, causing her tears to fall more quickly down her face.

"Just remember that I'll always be here for you when you need me. Always."

Before Elizabeth had a chance to respond, Todd had already turned and headed for the cashier. A few moments later the bells above the door chimed as Todd rushed out into the rain.

Elizabeth closed her eyes, hoping that when she opened them, Todd would be sitting across from her again, cracking jokes. But Todd was gone, really gone, and Tom was still outside on the bench.

Well, you've really done it this time, Elizabeth Wakefield, she scolded herself. *Now you've made Todd miserable too.* Todd, who she'd thought was the one for her. Todd, who'd helped her forget about Tom, if only for a brief while.

Elizabeth turned to the window, touching her fingers to it instinctively when she saw Tom curl up and bury his face in his hands. Elizabeth stroked the slick surface of the pane, imagining it was Tom's cheek. *Tom needs a friend, someone to hold him, but that someone isn't me. It's over.*

She jerked back her hand. *It's* over. *I'll never forgive him for what he's done. Never.*

Elizabeth winced, her eyes stinging. She leaned her forehead against the cold, damp window and kept on looking through it, not caring that her tears were leaving long streaks down the fogged surface of the glass.

Chapter
Ten

Here goes nothing, Jessica thought, her heart racing like mad. She checked Mrs. Fox's business card for the right phone number and dialed it, clutching the receiver with hot, slippery hands. She slammed the phone down almost immediately. *I can't do this.*

Suddenly the image of a certain gorgeous, green-eyed, motorcycle-riding detective flashed before her. *Oh yes I can,* she told herself, picking up the phone and pressing redial. She sat down daintily on Elizabeth's bed. On the other end of the wire the telephone rang once, twice, a third time, and then . . .

"Hello?"

Jessica didn't realize how unprepared she was to hear that horrible, grating voice again. Her mouth opened, but no sound came out.

"Hello!" Mrs. Fox's tone sharpened even more, much to Jessica's amazement.

"Hi," Jessica blurted. "This is J—uh, Margaret. We met the other day when I crashed—I mean, left a teeny tiny little ding in your car."

"Oh, it's *you*," Mrs. Fox responded derisively.

"I've been meaning to call sooner, Mrs.—uh, *Ms.* Fox. I just wanted to apologize for our little misunderstanding."

"Mm-hmm."

Jessica crossed her fingers, hoping that Mrs. Fox would apologize right back and laugh off the whole incident. After all, it was only the polite thing to do. But there was dead silence on the other end of the line.

Jessica took a deep breath. "Like I said, I'm *apologizing* for what happened," she repeated, struggling to keep her voice even. "I wasn't acting like myself. I'm normally not that, um, *vocal*. But I was just so upset—"

"*You* were upset?" Mrs. Fox broke in, sounding enraged. "How do you think *I* felt, having some reckless idiot damage my *brand-new* car!"

"Excuse me?" Jessica jumped to her feet, stunned. "This whole thing is *your* fault. I happen to be an excellent driver. I just didn't expect to see anyone *parked* on the *freeway!*"

"Well, you should have been keeping your eyes on the road. What were you doing? Your *hair?*"

"What were *you* doing?" Jessica shouted. "Looking for your brain?"

"Young lady, I believe this conversation is finished," Mrs. Fox said icily. "If I *ever* need to speak with you again, *I* will call *you*."

"Don't bother," Jessica snapped, just as the dial tone started buzzing in her ear.

Jessica slammed down the receiver and pointed at it. "Ha! That'll teach *you* to mess with a pro!" She jumped on her bed and did a victory dance. "When it comes to verbal battle, Jessica Wakefield *rules!*"

But reality sank in with irritating swiftness. "Wait a minute. What was I thinking? I just told off Nick's mother. Nick's *mother!*" She began to panic. "Oh no, not *again!*"

Jessica covered her face with her hands and flopped down on her bed. "I'm sunk. Totally dead in the water." She groaned, throwing her comforter over her as if she could safely hide under it forever.

"OK, girl, calm down. You can work this out," Jessica assured herself, grabbing her teddy bear for comfort. "First things first. You'll have to cancel dinner—again."

Jessica picked at the bear's ear and shook her head at her own advice. "But it's only a couple of hours away. What kind of excuse can I make this time? Will anyone even *believe* me?"

Let's face it, her voice echoed in her head, *you can't keep avoiding this meeting forever.* She got out from under her comforter and angrily threw the teddy bear across the room. It bounced off the wall and landed squarely in her empty wastebasket. *Wow, two points,* she thought, momentarily distracted.

Jessica sat and stared blankly into space for a few minutes. *All I can do is stall,* she finally decided. *Because if I don't plan my steps perfectly, the Fox family dinner could end up turning into a We-Hate-Jessica-Wakefield party.*

I must have rocks in my head, Nick Fox thought as he gunned his big Triumph motorcycle and raced onto the freeway. He knew he was going a little fast; to a police detective like himself, that was all part of a day's work. But tonight a slightly alien force was pushing him above the speed limit—plain, ordinary, household anxiety.

Not just rocks in my head, he mused, *but giant boulders.* As much as he wanted to deny it he was convinced that his mother and Jessica would get along like nitro and glycerine. Sure, his mother could be charming and sweet—but only when she felt like it. Most of the time Mrs. Fox was a real live pistol—hard to please and quick to anger.

Which was why his dad had ordered a special vanity plate for her new Lexus. Trouble was the perfect handle for his mother. Somehow he was sure that once his mother and Jessica were put in the same room, there wouldn't be just simple fireworks. No, there would be the kind of explosion that made dinosaurs extinct.

Nick's plan had always been to introduce his mother to the woman he was dating only in an absolute emergency or right before he said, "I do." He figured it was just safer that way. But he didn't want to be proven right—not tonight.

He sighed as he made the final turn into the SVU campus. The truth was, Jessica was special to him—very special. He was madly, passionately in love with her. The last thing he wanted was another obstacle in their relationship—the undercover drug sting fiasco was bad enough.

Nick's stomach turned at the memory of seeing Jessica waste away in a jail cell. He still felt guilty over putting her there—all because he didn't trust her when she swore she was innocent. He knew he had a lot to make up for. Nick had no choice but to give in when Jessica asked to reschedule the dinner.

Admit it, Fox, she's one of a kind, he told himself. *What other woman would do the kinds of things Jessica's done? She's impulsive, fearless, and willful. And you adore her.* If Jessica and Mrs. Fox could just get through the evening without scratching each other's eyes out, Nick would be satisfied.

Nick swung up to Dickenson Hall, parked the Triumph, and hurried inside. He ran his hand over his thick brown hair and straightened the sleeves of his black silk dress shirt. Nick was well aware he'd need to look his very best next to Jessica. Not only was she a natural beauty, but she also knew how to dress. When Jessica went all out, she was a total, knock-you-to-your-knees stunner.

Nick knocked on the door, his lips curving in anticipation. Would she be wearing that little black dress? Or maybe those slinky silver pants . . .

The door flung open to reveal Jessica in a long terry-cloth robe with big, fuzzy slippers on her feet. Her eyes widened pitifully beneath the ice pack she held to her forehead.

Shocked, Nick stared at her, struggling to speak coherently. "What's going on, Jess? Why aren't you dressed?"

"Come in," she said, grabbing Nick's arm. She shut the door and hastily perched on a chair, motioning for him to sit down on the chair next to her.

Nick remained standing, crossing his arms in front of him. *This had better be good,* he thought angrily.

Jessica's blue-green eyes pleaded with him. "I tried calling you before, Nick, but you didn't answer." She adjusted the ice pack against her forehead and tucked her uncombed hair behind an ear. Jessica's disheveled appearance made her seem a lot younger than her eighteen years and a lot more fragile than the Jessica Wakefield Nick knew and loved.

She's probably looking like that on purpose, Nick thought bitterly. He hated being jerked around.

Jessica pinched the bridge of her nose with her free hand. "I have another one of those terrible migraines. I'm sorry, Nick, but I can't go to dinner tonight."

"Oh, come *on*, Jess—"

Jessica held out one hand in appeasement. "I really want to, but I feel *sooo* miserable. I wouldn't make good company."

Nick couldn't help noticing how Jessica dropped her gaze and fidgeted in her chair after making her apology. Something was wrong—something that couldn't be cured with aspirin. Maybe she'd changed her mind about meeting his parents. Maybe she'd changed her mind about *him*.

"I'm not into mind games, Jessica," he said harshly. "I won't play them. If you want out of this relationship, then have the guts to tell me. Stop making up excuses."

"I'm *not* making up excuses!" Jessica wailed, dropping the ice pack to the floor and springing to her feet. "I don't want to break up! I never said a word about breaking up! Why are you saying such mean things to me . . . when . . . when I feel so sick!" Her lower lip quivered, and her eyes started to fill with tears.

Nick felt his defenses drop instantly and reached out to pull Jessica into his arms. "I'm so sorry, Jess. Don't—don't cry, please."

As Jessica sobbed against Nick's shoulder he cursed himself for being so hardheaded. How could he accuse Jessica of lying like that?

"I'm sorry, sunshine," he whispered, brushing his lips against the top of her head. "I didn't mean to lose my temper. I'm just under a lot of pressure right now. Please understand."

Jessica sniffed loudly. "So you don't want to break up with me?"

"Absolutely not," Nick responded gently.

Jessica's arms tightened around his waist. "But you treated me like I was a criminal."

"I can't apologize enough." Nick tilted Jessica's chin up with one finger, forcing her to meet his eyes. "But you have to admit that it looks pretty suspicious. How am I supposed to explain to my folks that you have *another* headache?"

Jessica fluttered her long lashes and gazed straight back into his eyes. "Well, it's not like I can *control* my headaches, can I?"

"I know, I know," he muttered. But his mind was still in a whirl. No way were his folks going to buy another headache excuse. And even though he knew his mother usually made more threats than she made promises, she'd still said that she'd never want to meet Jessica if she didn't make it to the dinner tonight. Nick groaned. No way would he tell Jessica that his own mother said something like that about her—especially considering Jessica's condition. He didn't want to reveal anything about his mother that would scare her off completely.

A quick peck on the cheek jolted Nick from his worries. Jessica was smiling up at him weakly, the side of her face pressed against his chest.

"Nick, could we reschedule again?" she begged. "I know it's a lot to ask, but I really want to make this up to you and your parents."

"I'll see what I can do," he promised. "Don't worry, everything'll be fine."

"I'm glad, Nick. I know you can make it all better." Jessica let out a yawn. "Whoa, I'm feeling sleepy. Would you apologize to your parents for me, please? Tell them how sorry I am?"

"Sure," Nick said gently, stroking her hair. "Are you going to be all right? Do you need anything?"

"No, thanks." Jessica gave him a look of genuine gratitude. "I'll be OK."

"Good. Feel better, Jess." Nick gave her another quick kiss before heading out the door.

"Don't worry," he mocked himself as he walked

down the hall. *You've sure got everything under control, Fox—about as much as you would surfing a tidal wave. Except with a tidal wave, you'd have a slightly higher chance of coming out in one piece.*

"Is it safe to come in now?" Elizabeth asked, peeking into the room she shared with her sister. Jessica was sitting inside, alone, but she didn't respond.

"I guess the coast is clear," Elizabeth remarked, stepping past the door and walking over to her bed. Jessica didn't even look up.

Elizabeth shrugged and stretched out. Jessica had made a huge deal out of asking Elizabeth to hide out in the hallway, insisting she needed privacy while she talked to Nick. But now that Nick was gone, Jessica was acting as if she was in a trance. Elizabeth knew all too well that this wasn't normal Jessica behavior. If she and Nick had argued, Jessica would be bouncing off the walls angrily. If something truly wonderful had happened, she'd be bouncing off the walls happily.

Why should I be concerned? I've got my own mood swings to worry about, Elizabeth told herself as she rubbed her temples. What Elizabeth really wanted was to crawl into a nice, quiet, dark hole and stay there—for about a thousand years. Anything to get away from Tom Watts and Todd Wilkins and the pained expressions she'd put on both their faces.

I've hurt two people, Elizabeth realized, then shook her head. *No, not really. If Tom is miserable, it's his own fault. And what happened with Todd—that's all Tom's fault too.* Elizabeth was fighting to make her twisted logic work, but she was too distracted by an irritating noise. The sound of someone sighing loudly and repeatedly.

"What's wrong, Jessica?" Elizabeth said with slight impatience. "You sound like a beached whale. You didn't argue with Nick, did you?"

Jessica stared at her tragically. "How could you do that to me, Liz? How could you compare me to some huge old fish?"

"Mammal," Elizabeth corrected automatically. She studied her sister. Jessica *did* look pretty dejected, she had to admit.

"Whatever," Jessica said with disinterest. Suddenly she jumped to her feet with a dramatic flourish and posed in front of Elizabeth. "Pray tell, what am I wearing?"

Elizabeth narrowed her eyes. "My robe and my slippers," she answered wearily. She didn't even bother reprimanding her sister for borrowing her clothes. She was too interested in what Jessica was leading up to.

Jessica rolled her eyes. "You are so . . . so *practical,* Liz. Use your imagination. When have you ever seen me dressed like this?"

"Never," Elizabeth answered immediately. "Why, are you sick?"

Jessica twisted her face into a melodramatic pout. "Yes, I am. Heartsick!" She flopped back down on the bed and put an ice pack on her forehead.

"I thought you were OK, Jess. Why the ice pack?"

"I was using it to convince Nick I had a migraine," Jessica said calmly, dropping the ice pack over the side of the bed. It landed on top of a stack of old magazines.

"A migraine?" She scanned her sister's face. "A pretend migraine, I take it."

Jessica's trademark confidence seemed to drain out of her, right before Elizabeth's eyes. "Yup, I lied to Nick."

Elizabeth rolled her eyes and sat up. "Why, Jess? I thought you loved Nick. Why would you lie to him?"

"It was an emergency!"

Elizabeth's brows shot up toward her hairline. "An emergency? What happened *now*, Jessica? This wouldn't have anything to do with Mrs. Fox, would it?"

Jessica nodded solemnly. "I'm in a really bad jam, Liz, and it's getting worse. I don't know what I'm going to do."

"Tell me about it, Jess. I'm listening."

Jessica cleared her throat. "I did what you

said and sent Mrs. Fox a card and a gift, but what I didn't tell you—"

"Uh-oh. What else did you do, Jessica?"

"I was just trying to fix things, Liz, honestly." Jessica suddenly jumped to her feet. "You know what? I'm starved. Why don't we have some ice cream? I saw some butter pecan in the freezer."

"You're stalling, Jess," Elizabeth said with a sigh. "But the bad news can wait. I could go for a bowl of ice cream—more like ten bowls. Maybe all that sugar and cream will help us both."

"Why, is your love life as messed up as mine?" Jessica asked sympathetically as she walked to the minifridge and got the ice cream out of the tiny freezer. "Do tell."

"No, you have to finish telling me *your* story, Jess." Elizabeth walked over to the small table and sat down. "And I know you can dish and talk at the same time."

Jessica bit her lip as she dug in for the first scoop. "Well, when we had our accident, I gave Mrs. Fox my phone number. I never wrote down my name. So when I called, I told her my name was Margaret."

Elizabeth massaged her forehead. "Great, Jess. You're lying to Nick's mother too?"

"Lila told me to!" Jessica cried as she plunked two dishes of ice cream down on the table. "It seemed like the perfect plan at the time, but it turned out to be the worst mistake I could have made." She took a bite of her ice cream. "Ow! Ice cream headache."

"There you go, Jess. You really *do* have a headache now."

"Very funny, Liz. Anyway, when I called up Mrs. Fox to apologize, we ended up getting into a big fight. I think I really insulted her."

"*Jes*-si-ca," Elizabeth scolded. "Why can't you control your temper?"

Jessica stirred her ice cream into a soup. "I don't know. I guess because I was using someone else's name, I just felt like I could say anything to her." She put her spoon down on the table. "What am I going to do? I can't keep putting off Nick's parents like this. As long as we're still dating, I'll have to meet them eventually."

"But after you finally *do* meet them . . . ," Elizabeth began.

"Nick will probably want to break up with me. I know." Jessica shook her head. "It's a total no-win situation."

Elizabeth shrugged. "You need to come clean soon, Jess. Once the situation is out in the open, you'll be able to work it out. I'm sure his parents will understand."

"Thanks, but I don't believe it for a second. You've never talked to this woman, Liz. She's got a temper like you wouldn't believe. I've pretty much accepted failure already," Jessica said sadly. "What about you? What's going on in your life?"

"I wish I knew," Elizabeth whispered. She stared into her bowl of ice cream as if it would reveal the answer to her. "I thought I wanted to date Todd again, but . . ." Her voice trailed off.

"You said you *loved* Todd. You wanted to be with him," Jessica reminded her with a look of genuine concern.

Elizabeth shook her head. "I was being too hasty. That was before I saw Tom—"

"You saw Tom? What happened?"

"Nothing . . . and everything," Elizabeth said. "I only saw him out a window while I was out with Todd, but it brought everything back. I was just fooling myself, Jess. I'm not ready to move on."

Jessica frowned. "Don't give up on Todd too fast, Liz. Todd's a hunk, and he's *crazy* about you."

"It's hopeless. I can't love both Tom and Todd, can I?" Elizabeth stared dejectedly at her twin sister; she could tell that Jessica's sad face mirrored her own perfectly. Simultaneously they turned to eat the rest of their ice cream. The silence was disturbed only by the sound of spoons scraping against dishes.

Jessica got to her feet. "I don't know about you, but I could really use a long, hot shower. Then I'm going to walk off that ice cream."

"I think I'll just study for a while," Elizabeth said, slowly picking up the dishes.

"Cheer up, Liz," Jessica said, pausing at the door with her shower basket in hand. "Our lives are so pathetic right now, they can only get better."

After Jessica left, Elizabeth dropped the dishes back down on the table and dashed over to her bed, trying to ignore the deep depression she felt coming on. Why couldn't she just put her problems aside the way Jessica could? Her life was like a nonstop string of *I Love Lucy* episodes. Crazy, irresponsible, and erratic. But Jessica's life was never desperate—not like Elizabeth's.

Maybe this is what I deserve, Elizabeth thought. She buried her face in her pillow and wept as if her heart would break. She loved two men, but she was utterly and completely alone.

Chapter
Eleven

"She's not coming! I knew it!" Mrs. Fox cried the moment Nick walked through the front door. "I had a feeling your mystery girlfriend wasn't going to show up, and my instincts are never wrong."

"Now, Rhoda . . ."

"Oh, come on, Ben! You're just angry because you lost our bet!"

"*Mom,*" Nick protested. "You were actually *betting* on Jessica?"

"Like I said," Mrs. Fox declared triumphantly, "my instincts are never wrong."

Nick cast a longing look at the doorway he just walked through. It would only take about five seconds to turn around and make a run for freedom.

Mr. Fox sighed. "What happened, Nick?" he asked quietly.

Nick turned around and took a good look at his parents, who were dressed to the nines. They were all set to go to the Jambalaya House. Changing reservations hadn't been an easy task—the exclusive restaurant was usually booked weeks in advance. But his mother had been awfully persuasive. Still, Nick wondered what the odds would be for another try.

Here goes nothing, he thought, taking a deep breath. "Well, Mom, it looks like you were right after all. Jessica was dying to come, but she got another one of those headaches. She's very upset and very sorry."

His mother's face was openly skeptical; his father's, sympathetic. *Typical,* thought Nick.

"I was the one who told her to stay home and sleep it off," Nick continued, pulling at his collar a little. It seemed to be getting tighter. "I mean, we could always make it another night, right?"

Mrs. Fox snorted. "Very interesting, Nick. Good story, but I think I know what's really going on here."

"C'mon, Rhoda, let's give the poor girl a break," Mr. Fox interrupted. "Jessica may be a little—*erratic,* but we shouldn't make snap judgments. Perhaps she has a few emotional problems, and we shouldn't—"

Mrs. Fox abruptly turned on her heel and walked into the living room to take a seat on the sofa. "You're soft-pedaling the issue, Ben. The girl is a flake, and you know it. She obviously wants attention and sympathy. What other explanation can there be for all of these headaches and canceled dinners!"

Mr. Fox headed for his favorite easy chair. "That might be true, but we don't want to hurt Nick's feelings—"

"Hold it right there, guys!" Nick bellowed, bringing the slander to a halt. His mother and father stared at him, amazed. "Jessica is *not* a flake, and she doesn't have emotional problems. The only thing wrong with her is a simple headache. She can't help that." He could feel himself getting overheated, so he paused to unbutton his collar. "Please give her another chance. Once you meet her, you'll see how great she is. She's beautiful, dynamic, and—"

"Insipid?" Mrs. Fox finished for him. She reached behind the sofa and, with a flourish, pulled out a garish pink-and-white stuffed teddy bear. The bear was clutching a big heart in its paws.

Nick leaned forward to read the message: I'm beary, beary sorry. An involuntary groan slipped from his lips.

"My feelings exactly!" his mother said succinctly. "What kind of a girl would send something so sappy and sickening? You should see the card that came with it."

"Never mind." Nick shook his head despite himself. What could have possessed Jessica to send something so sickly sweet? "I'm sure Jessica meant well, Mom. Can't you give her a break?"

His mother sighed and dropped the bear onto the sofa. "I'm only looking out for your best interests, Nicky."

Nick bit back another groan. He hated that idiotic nickname.

"I just can't picture you with that kind of girl. The sugary type was never right for you." Mrs. Fox's eyes suddenly sparkled. "But I happen to know a woman—high-spirited, stubborn, and wild—who would be perfect for you."

"Mother . . . ," Nick muttered.

"Rhoda . . . ," Mr. Fox chimed in at the exact same moment.

Mrs. Fox ignored them both. "Her name is Margaret. She's the one who trashed my Lexus. She called me earlier, and boy, did she read me the riot act. She's a regular wildcat, Nicky. Perfect for you. If you give me a minute or two, I can find her phone number. . . ."

Enough is enough, Nick thought, waving his arms wildly. "Look, Mom, please stop joking around—"

"I'm not joking," she interrupted. "I'm completely serious."

"No, please, listen to me. I really—I really

care about Jessica." *I'll say,* Nick added silently. *If I weren't crazy about Jessica, I wouldn't put myself through the wringer like this.*

"The bottom line is, I really want you to meet her," Nick pleaded. "I want you to like her. And I think you will."

Mr. Fox watched his son closely. "We'd be happy to postpone dinner until Jessica is feeling better. We're very eager to meet her, aren't we, Rhoda?" He shot Mrs. Fox a pointed look.

Nick's mother glowered for a moment, then shrugged. "Fine. What day? Sometime next year, perhaps?"

"Friday night," Nick said quickly. *And Jess, you'd better show this time,* he thought savagely, *or else . . .*

Or else nothing, Fox, he answered himself. *You love her, and nothing's going to change that.*

"Just do it," urged Jamie Lynn. "You'll feel better once you hear Todd's voice." Jamie Lynn was doing stomach crunches on the floor while Gin-Yung sat huddled at her desk, her dark head bent over a pile of papers.

Gin-Yung stared at her notes. Her carefully printed words were just a jumble to her tired eyes.

"Come—on—Gin—Yung," Jamie Lynn choked out between reps.

"No, maybe I should wait," Gin-Yung said

hesitantly. "Todd never even returned my last call." Gin-Yung looked up at the ceiling and swallowed hard. She couldn't give in to tears now, not with Jamie Lynn in the room.

Jamie Lynn panted as she counted. "Eighty-one, eighty-two, eighty-three . . ."

"I don't know how you can do that, Jamie Lynn. It makes me tired just watching you."

"You—get—used—to—it." Jamie Lynn came to a stop. "Let's not change the subject, Gin-Yung. What if Todd never got your message? Those dumb old machines are unreliable. They break down all the time."

"I guess," Gin-Yung stalled. She examined what she'd written on the pages in front of her, trying in vain to get excited about her work. It was hot news: an American girls' soccer team, the Spirit of Massachusetts, had won a major championship and was in London challenging the Whippets, a top British girls' team. Gin-Yung should have been enthusiastic, even ecstatic. This kind of thing made front-page news in Europe.

But nothing seemed to interest her now, except for getting in touch with Todd. Gin-Yung's eyes grew damp. *Todd may still matter to me, but the big question is, Do I still matter to Todd?* Suddenly she straightened in her seat. *Snap out of it,* she told herself. Self-pity wasn't her scene—no way. She'd go to the game, sit in the front row, and act like nothing was wrong. *That's it. Pull yourself together. You can't fall apart now.*

"You know what, Jamie Lynn," Gin-Yung said confidently, "you're absolutely right. I *will* call Todd." She stacked her papers into a neat pile and stood up. "Whether he got my message or not, I still have to talk to him."

Jamie Lynn got to her feet, grimacing as she snatched up her towel and robe. "Ugh, I need a shower. That'll give you some privacy in the meantime."

"Thanks."

Jamie Lynn paused at the door to smile encouragingly at Gin-Yung. "Don't forget that Todd is lucky to have a girl like you. You tell him I said so." She winked before heading out into the hall.

I wish I had her energy and her confidence too, Gin-Yung thought morosely. *I'm at a loss for both right now.* Quickly she picked up the phone and dialed before she lost her nerve.

Gin-Yung didn't realize she'd been holding her breath until she heard Todd answer, "Yeah?" Then she sighed with relief, her entire body seeming to collapse.

"Todd, it's me," Gin-Yung said, forcing cheer into her voice. Her trembling fingers clutched the phone so tightly, she could feel it quivering against her ear.

"Oh, Gin-Yung, hi," he said. But to Gin-Yung's sensitive ears, he sounded disappointed. Was he hoping it was someone else?

She steadied herself and sat down at her desk. "I missed you and decided, what the heck? Why not blow my budget and call again!" Her own voice sounded tinny and loud to her. But she clenched her jaw, determined to forge ahead.

"So . . . how've you been?" Todd's tone seemed distant in a way that suggested more than just the miles between them. He paused, as if struggling to think of something else to say. "You were kind of worn out last time we spoke. Are you feeling any better?"

Gin-Yung ignored the question. There was something more pressing on her mind. "Uh, Todd, I was wondering if you got my message the other day. Was your machine working?"

"Yeah, I'm sorry," he mumbled nervously. "I meant to call you, but I got tied up with practice. You know how it is."

Gin-Yung stared down at her loafers. A wave of cold desolation made her shiver. *Yes, I know how it is. You're losing interest in me—that's obvious.* She rubbed her shoe heel against the hem of her slacks. There had to be some topic that would pique Todd's attention.

"Guess what?" she asked, striving to sound lively and excited. "That Massachusetts team made it to the finals and is going to play the Whippets. I get to cover the whole series." Maybe that would wake Todd up.

"That's terrific," Todd answered. "Good for you." Then he went silent.

Gin-Yung's heart sank. This conversation was completely stalled—a total failure. Todd acted as if he'd rather be anywhere but on the telephone with her.

Todd cleared his throat. The forceful sound stood out in sharp contrast to Todd's weak, disinterested conversation. "Say, Gin-Yung, I hate to say this, but I have a ton of studying to do. I really have to hit the books."

"OK," Gin-Yung replied, dejected.

"Take care of yourself," Todd said quickly.

"See you later," she mumbled, even though she was sure Todd must have rushed to hang up before she even signed off. Gin-Yung replaced the receiver and sank lower in her desk chair. *Jamie Lynn was wrong,* she thought with a long sigh. *I don't feel a bit better. As a matter of fact, that call made me feel a thousand times worse.*

Todd sounded so cold and aloof. Was he seeing someone else? Even though they'd agreed to date other people, Gin-Yung never imagined that Todd would stop caring about her. That wasn't his style. She was sure their relationship would be safe.

Gin-Yung got up and staggered to her bed. She dropped down and buried her face in her pillow, not even bothering to take off her shoes. If Todd was dating someone, he would tell her, wouldn't he? They had promised each other to be truthful and open.

Gin-Yung tried to imagine going home and learning that Todd was in love with another woman. *No,* she decided, *that can't be what's going on.* Todd wouldn't keep Gin-Yung in the dark. He was a kind, caring person. *The answer is, long-distance relationships are difficult, period.*

Gin-Yung sighed softly. *Maybe Todd is feeling as uncertain as I am.* She nodded. *Now, that makes sense. Todd might be having doubts about* me.

Gin-Yung pulled up her spread and covered herself. *Even so,* she mused, *I'm glad I didn't tell him what's really going on here. Because right now, Todd wouldn't be able to handle it.*

Elizabeth was entwined in Todd's arms, laughing cruelly. "You've lost me forever, Tom," she chortled with glee. "Forever!" She cuddled up to Todd, who smirked and said, "You're a loser, Watts, and you always will be."

Mercifully the dream dissolved, and Tom let out a moan of relief. *What a nightmare,* he thought. *Now, if I could just get a few winks of dream-free shut-eye, I'll be satisfied.* But something started ringing . . . and ringing.

"Go away," Tom mumbled, burying his head under the quilt. Yet the ringing didn't stop. In fact, it grew more insistent. And louder. Tom growled in frustration. Couldn't a man get a little restful sleep—even if he happened to be skipping all his classes on a Thursday afternoon?

Now the ringing was joined by a pounding noise. Whoever was on the other side of the door was going at it with both barrels. He closed his eyes and covered his ears, but it was no use.

Tom rubbed his eyes and struggled out of bed. For a second he was disoriented, forgetting he'd been napping in the Conroy guest room. The large, airy room was foreign to his sleep-befuddled eyes. He rubbed them vigorously and staggered down the hall.

"I'm coming!" he shouted. "Keep your pants on, will you!" *Why couldn't someone else answer the stupid door,* he thought with irritation. Then he remembered that Mary and Jake were playing outside so he could have some peace and quiet.

Even after he yelled, the noise kept on going. Tom could feel his blood pressure rise. *Someone is bent on driving me insane. It obviously isn't enough that I'm more depressed and miserable than I've ever been in my entire life—so miserable that I'm actually hiding out here at the Conroys' instead of going to class.*

Angrily he grabbed the doorknob and yanked open the door. "For Pete's sake, you're going to break it down," Tom yelled. "What's your problem, any—" He stopped short, gaping.

An absolute vision stood before him.

Tom blinked. It was the dark-haired beauty he'd bumped into—literally—a few days ago.

Tom ran his hands over his hair and quickly tucked his navy cotton shirt into his jeans. *At least I'm dressed decently,* he thought, dazed. *What if I'd answered the door in old sweats—or my boxers.* He winced at the image. Still, he knew he looked pretty out of it.

The vision was speaking. Her voice was like polished silk rubbing against his bare skin. "Hi. I'm Dana Upshaw," she said breathily. "I'm here for Mary's cello lesson." Dana held up a large, shiny black case for emphasis. It was almost as tall as she was. "Was I knocking too loudly? I thought the kids might have their headphones on."

Tom just kept gaping at her.

"I hope I didn't disturb you." Dana raised her large hazel eyes slowly, scanning him thoroughly. A warm smile spread across her face.

I guess I don't look as bad I thought, Tom assured himself.

It finally occurred to Tom that he had been standing there like a mute, goggle-eyed dolt. When he rubbed his stubbly jaw, he vaguely realized that he needed a shave. *Maybe Dana likes the five o'clock shadow look,* he thought. Casually Tom leaned against the door frame and said, "I'm Tom Watts."

"I know," Dana said. "The last time I ran into you, Mary and Jake couldn't sing your praises loudly enough. Jake practically worships the ground you walk on."

Tom laughed softly. "Mary can't stop talking about you either," he added, discreetly taking note of Dana's beautiful face and her curvaceous body, which was flawlessly showcased in a watermelon pink tank top and white Capri pants. A pair of cat's-eye sunglasses rested atop Dana's thick mane of mahogany hair. To Tom, she looked like a Hollywood glamour girl, a fifties starlet. *Very quirky—and classy too,* Tom thought. *And very, very sexy.* "From all the good things she's told me, I couldn't believe you were real. But here you are."

"Here *we* are," Dana replied, her tone echoing his—low and sultry. When their eyes locked, Tom felt his mouth go dry.

"Mary's been asking me to go to her concert," Tom said, gesturing to the cello case in Dana's hand. "I've never seen her play onstage, so I'm looking forward to it."

"I think you'll enjoy it, Tom. Really." Dana laid a cool hand on Tom's arm and leaned closer. Her crisp perfume teased Tom's senses. "The cello is a passionate and beautiful instrument. There's nothing else like it."

"In that case I'm *really* looking forward to it," Tom assured her. "Will you be playing at the concert too?"

"Oh no, this is for students only," Dana replied. "I do play at other concerts, though."

"I'd love to see you perform. You're probably like this Jacqueline person Mary keeps raving about."

Dana shook her head, her expression turning reverent. "Jacqueline Du Pré was peerless. I could only dream."

"I know what you mean. Edward R. Murrow was the greatest journalist who ever lived. I always tell myself, 'If I could be even one-fifth as good as Edward R. Murrow . . .'" He trailed off, suddenly reminded that Elizabeth felt the same way. *You need to forget about the past, Watts,* he lectured himself. *Take a look in front of you. This could be your big chance.*

"Speaking of journalism," Tom continued, glancing at his watch, "I'm due at WSVU in less than an hour."

Speak up now, a voice inside him said, *or forever hold your peace.*

"Uh, Dana," he continued, "this may sound a little crazy, but . . . are you free tomorrow night? I know you might be all booked up and everything, seeing as how it's a Friday night, but—"

"I'm not booked at all," Dana interrupted him, her hazel eyes sparkling. "I'd love to go out, if that's what you're getting at."

Tom nodded enthusiastically, and Dana's face turned impish. "But it's on *one* condition," she said.

"Name it," Tom said, grinning in anticipation.

"Could you let me in the house so I can give Mary her cello lesson?" She crooked an eyebrow, then laughed a little. Her laugh was bright and chimelike.

"You got it," Tom said, grateful she had a sense of humor. As he stepped aside to let Dana in, he felt a few soft, mahogany tendrils brush his upper arm. *Today is my lucky day,* he realized with satisfaction. *Watch out, Elizabeth Wakefield. You may think you've done me in, but look what I've found— the perfect woman to help me forget you for good.*

Chapter Twelve

"That does it," Elizabeth said out loud. She closed her literature book with a loud snap. There were only a few other people nearby, but they all turned around to stare at her.

Elizabeth felt her face heat up. She'd forgotten she wasn't alone. The snack bar was so quiet on Friday nights that the die-hard scholars often used it as a study lounge. The place was calm, well lit, and unexciting.

Unexciting, just like me, Elizabeth thought with disgust. *Elizabeth Wakefield, who always plays it safe. Elizabeth Wakefield, who's about as fascinating as cold oatmeal.* She knew she was being hard on herself but felt she needed the wake-up call. After all, it was Friday night. The beginning of the weekend. A night full of sweet promise; a night when romances are born—

supposedly. Instead Elizabeth was sitting by herself, drinking black coffee and reading a textbook.

The realization made Elizabeth spring to her feet. She tightened her ponytail and slapped on her baseball cap. She gathered all her study materials and stuffed them in her backpack. Then she stood for a moment and surveyed the snack bar. It was eerily silent, like a still-life painting. She shuddered. *Maybe I'm becoming petrified too, like old wood.* Elizabeth took a deep breath as she threw the pack over her shoulder. *One thing is for sure—I can't keep letting men ruin my happiness. I doubt either Tom or Todd is spending their Friday night moping around.*

No more drooping around like the last rose of summer, she told herself as she hurried outside. It was time to put a little pizzazz and pleasure back into her life.

Elizabeth walked directionlessly across the quad. The sky was darkening rapidly, and the air was cool. Elizabeth had goose bumps. She was wearing only a short-sleeved tunic over leggings and hadn't thought to bring a jacket. All around her couples paraded by, keeping each other warm. Elizabeth tried to ignore them.

Heaving a sigh of relief, she spotted an events board posted outside the student union. Elizabeth stepped closer, hoping against hope that she'd find something interesting to do. A big white posterboard announced a poëtry reading on campus. The work of Elizabeth's favorite poet, Maya Angelou, was going to be featured. And it was tonight!

Elizabeth was galvanized. Why not call Nina? She was probably out with her boyfriend, but it wouldn't hurt to check. Elizabeth raced to a nearby pay phone and pledged to herself she would go to the reading even if Nina was busy. Luckily she got ahold of Nina almost instantly.

"I'd love to go," Nina said eagerly. "Anything's better than hanging around my room. For the last hour the chips and cookies in the vending machine have been calling my name. Getting out of here would be a wise move." Nina chuckled.

Elizabeth smiled. "Then it's a good thing I called. It's my mission to rescue you from the lurid temptation of the calorie."

"I adore Maya Angelou's work," Nina enthused. "She's wonderful. I love 'I Know Why the Caged Bird Sings.' It's my favorite."

"Mine too," Elizabeth agreed. "But where's Bryan tonight?"

Nina sighed. "You know Bryan—work, work, work. He's concentrating on his big rally, so I really can't blame him."

Elizabeth giggled. "But part of you does."

"Right," Nina responded without missing a beat.

"Well, then, tonight should be perfect. What

could be better than two women enjoying a night of culture together?"

"Ab-so-*lute*-ly nothing."

"Maybe we should ban men as a topic of discussion for tonight, at least," Elizabeth suggested.

"Fine with me," Nina agreed. "It's a girls' night out, then?"

"Perfect," Elizabeth said succinctly. *Who needs guys anyway,* she added silently to herself.

"Maybe if I told Nick I had temporary amnesia . . . that I forgot all about our dinner tonight . . ." Jessica brightened for a moment. Then her shoulders drooped as she realized he'd never believe her in a million years. Jessica stared into the antique mirror hanging above her dresser. Her reflection showed a very pretty blond girl with a very worried expression on her face.

Jessica studied herself carefully. This time she had opted for a simple gold chain instead of Elizabeth's cameo necklace. That cameo was jinxed as far as she was concerned. But she was giving her pink dress and jacket another try. Still, she was fretting. What if the outfit was jinxed too? Jessica didn't have a choice but to wear it. She couldn't afford to go shopping again, and nothing else looked right.

Her long golden hair hung loose except for

two tiny barrettes in the front. Jessica added a touch of rose-colored lipstick to her mouth and frowned. She looked good, but what did it matter? Once Nick's mother took a gander at her, she was dead meat.

Jessica groaned out loud and sank onto the bed. *There has to be a way out of this dinner. Maybe another headache,* she thought suddenly, then sank back down. *No, Nick would think I was seriously sick and cart me off to the nearest hospital.*

There was a knock at the door. Jessica froze and stared down at her pink pumps. "Doom," she whispered under her breath. "Doom is at my door."

"Jess, open up." Nick sounded sexily impatient.

Jessica leaped to her feet and pasted a smile on her face. "Well, here goes nothing," she whispered to herself in desperation.

When Jessica opened the door, Nick looked stunning, but concerned. "Jessica, what's wrong? You look like you've seen a ghost or something." Nick's crisp green shirt brought out the jade color in his eyes and showed off his lean, muscled physique. His thick brown hair was brushed sleekly back. Despite his frown, he was still heart-stoppingly handsome.

Jessica stared back at him. *I can't lose Nick; I just can't.*

Nick drew her to him, sliding his arm across

her shoulders. "What's up, sunshine? You're acting like you've just lost your best friend." His eyes were dark with worry.

Jessica inhaled Nick's fresh, tangy cologne and slipped her arms around his waist. When she leaned against his chest and closed her eyes, she could practically feel the impatience radiating from him.

"C'mon, Jess, what's going on?" Nick was starting to sound a little . . . suspicious, maybe? *But he can't know,* Jessica reassured herself frantically. *There is no way he can know about the accident.*

She forced herself to open her eyes and gaze deeply into his. "Nothing's going on, Nick," she replied sweetly. "I've just missed you. I hardly get to see you these days."

"Now, whose fault is that?" His right brow lifted incredulously.

Her giggle came out high and strained. "Mine, I know." She smiled up at him. "Shouldn't we be going? I don't want to keep your parents waiting. I've done that enough lately."

Nick nodded. "You're right. Let's get this show on the road."

In minutes they were tooling down the highway in Nick's black Camaro. It was a particularly windy day, which explained why he wasn't riding his motorcycle. Jessica was relieved; the last thing she needed was messy hair. Since Nick's mother only had seen Jessica with a totally wrecked 'do, Jessica hoped that maybe Mrs. Fox wouldn't recognize her with a neater look.

As the Camaro zoomed past houses, gas stations, and shopping centers Jessica longingly watched them pass by, wishing desperately that she could go to any one of those places instead of to the Foxes'. Jessica was hurtling toward disaster, and there wasn't a thing she could do about it. *Maybe I should have told Nick the truth earlier,* she thought. *But it doesn't matter now. I'm trapped—trapped and doomed.*

"You're awfully quiet, Jess," Nick remarked without taking his eyes from the road. "I hope you're not nervous."

"I'm not," Jessica said in a hushed voice.

"Just don't make too big a deal out of this, OK?" He shot her a quick glance. "Remember, I told you they're a little . . . difficult. So don't expect too much."

Jessica stiffened in her seat. Nick acted as if his parents were going to hate her no matter what. How unfair! *They don't even know that I'm the woman who crashed into their Lexus—yet. Then they'll really have a reason to hate me.*

"Thanks a lot, Nick," she retorted sarcastically. "I'm not a monster, you know. Why shouldn't they like me?"

Nick sighed and scratched his jaw. Jessica

knew that meant he was stalling. "Uh, Jessica . . . did you send my mother a stuffed bear? She got it the other day, and—"

Jessica didn't like Nick's tone one bit. "Yes, I did. I sent her a card too, to apologize for canceling out," Jessica responded in a tight, sharp voice. "Why? What about it?"

"The thing is, Jess, my mother is not the kind of a person who goes in for . . . *sappy* stuff like that. Why would *you* send something like that anyway? I didn't think that was your style."

Jessica gasped. "Of all the nerve! Your mother complained about a *gift* that I sent her?"

Nick rolled his eyes. "I told you she was a difficult person. She's not the hearts-and-flowers type. I'm sorry I told you, but—"

Jessica cut him off. "*You're* sorry!" she screeched. *How* dare *Mrs. Fox insult my gift!* Jessica thought, her mind blazing. *That woman is evil!*

"Look, Jessica—"

"No. *You* look. *I'm* sorry, OK? I'm sorry I even bothered to send a nice gift to your mother. In fact, I'm sorry I ever asked for this dinner in the first place. Now if you'll excuse me, I'm getting out of this car—*right now!*"

Jessica flung off her seat belt, her hands shaking violently as she grabbed the door handle of the door and popped the lock. The car was flying at top speed when Jessica cracked open the door. A gust of air rushed inside.

"I'm not staying where I'm not wanted," Jessica shouted hysterically over the loud, vacuumlike hiss. "I'm out of here!"

"Jessica, stop!" With one arm Nick reached across the seat and savagely yanked the door shut.

"Watch it, Nick! You almost snagged my jacket!" Jessica cried, giving Nick her most furious pout.

"Are you *nuts?*" Nick exclaimed as he used one hand to fasten Jessica's seat belt with quick, angry motions. "We're going over sixty miles an hour! You could have been killed!"

Jessica tossed her head. Even though she appeared confident and unruffled on the outside, she was still trembling inside. "Maybe I'd rather die than eat dinner with people who despise me."

He groaned and slammed the steering wheel with his fist. "You take the cake, Jess, you really do. First you strong-arm me into *inviting* you to this dinner, and now you want to back out of it?"

Jessica jutted out her lower lip and stared straight ahead.

"Well, forget it, Jess. You demanded this dinner, and you're going to get it. Understand?"

Jessica shot him an indignant look. "You don't have to sound so bossy! You're not my probation officer or anything."

Nick tightened his jaw and muttered under his breath, "You're lucky I'm not."

Jessica refused to speak, especially considering the thundercloud expression on Nick's face. Tensely she chewed her cuticle and resigned herself to despair. Meeting Nick's parents was supposed to bring her and Nick closer. But instead it was messing everything up!

The best she could hope for was that Mrs. Fox was either extremely nearsighted or that she'd been too angry during the accident to get a good look at Jessica. Otherwise this was destined to be the worst family dinner in recorded history!

"It's amazing that we just met, Tom," Dana gushed. "I feel like I've known you forever." She glided beside him, her long dark hair swinging. The brilliant, starlit sky rose like a velvet canopy above their heads. The SVU campus was alive with sound. Music poured from stereos in nearby dorms; laughter and chatter filled the quad. Frat houses were rocking, charging the atmosphere with excitement and vitality.

Tom smiled down at her. "Me too," he said softly, wishing he really meant it. Tom was happy to have found a woman—a gorgeous, talented woman—to keep his mind off Elizabeth. But even though he and Dana were having a fabulous time together, Tom wasn't so sure if his idea was a good one.

"It's great to get away from studies and cello practice," Dana added. She shot him a quick look from under her lashes. "I'm so glad you asked me out."

"Yeah, well, I needed the break too," Tom said.

"Not that I mind practicing the cello. I love it, actually. I'm always hearing music in my head," Dana confessed.

Tom gave her an understanding look. "I do that too. Not with music, of course. But I see interesting stories everywhere I go, whether I'm looking for them or not."

Dana glanced at him through her lashes. "Do you see an interesting story in me?" she asked, her voice soft and seductive. The look she gave him sent shivers through his body.

"You?" he asked, allowing himself to give in to Dana's flirtations a little. "You're worth at least a whole book."

"Hey," she murmured, moving close enough to brush his arm with hers. "I like that answer."

Tom closely examined the woman who walked beside him. Dana looked supremely tempting in a short black knit halter dress. She wore dangling silver earrings that flashed enticingly against her glossy mane of hair. But even with her good looks, quick wit, and intelligence, it was Dana's slyly provocative behavior that was making Tom warm up to her more easily than he expected.

"So you're a student at SVU too?" he asked after a short silence. "I haven't seen you around."

Dana nodded. "I'm a music major. I've been playing the cello my entire life." She flipped her hair over her shoulder. "Music has been a driving force for me. To play or to listen. It doesn't matter which. Music is what I live for."

"I've felt that way about journalism," Tom commented. "I guess you could say I have ink in my veins." He grinned and took Dana's arm as they crossed the lawn. It was dark, and the terrain was rough. Dana was a little unsteady in her high heels.

"It shows. I've seen those great reports that you did with Elizabeth Wakefield on WSVU," Dana mused. Her eyes were inquisitive as they scanned his face. "Weren't you dating her at one time?"

Tom stiffened, his smile slipping away. Elizabeth was the last topic he wanted to discuss tonight. "Yes," he answered shortly. "We used to." He scowled for a second, irritated that Dana had brought Elizabeth up. "But we're not anymore." Tom knew his tone was harsh, but he couldn't stop himself. Just the sound of Elizabeth's name could make him snap. "I'd rather not talk about her."

Dana rubbed his arm gently. "Then we don't have to," she said softly, casting a quick glance at Tom from under her lashes. "I didn't mean to upset you. You two were a famous couple around campus, that's all."

Tom didn't say anything. He stared straight ahead, trying to calm himself down.

Dana slipped her hand in his. Her skin felt smooth and warm to Tom's stiff fingers. "Why don't we just focus on us tonight and forget the rest of the world exists?" Dana asked, giving Tom's shoulder a squeeze with her free hand.

If only that were possible, Tom thought. "OK, Dana. Tell you what. I'll just try to concentrate on you tonight. You and nothing else." He entwined his fingers with Dana's and let the pressure of her hand soothe him.

"Hey, Tombo!" a familiar voice boomed through the darkness. As Danny Wyatt approached with a tentative smile on his face Tom felt a twinge of discomfort. Since the embarrassing scene at the Delta Chi party, Tom had been avoiding him as much as he could.

"Hi, Tom," a soft, feminine voice echoed Danny's. Isabella Ricci, looking elegant and beautiful as always, was walking beside Danny.

She was in a scarlet jacket and pants that contrasted brilliantly with her black hair and creamy skin. Her gray eyes were curious as they traveled back and forth from Tom to Dana.

Danny was less subtle. "Aren't you going to introduce us?" he quizzed, his eyebrows raised slightly.

Tom put his arm around Dana's waist and smiled broadly at Danny and Isabella. "This is Dana Upshaw. She teaches my new half sister the cello, and she likes Maya Angelou's poetry as much as I do."

"What a coincidence," Danny mentioned. "Iz and I are going to the reading too."

Tom inwardly groaned. He liked Danny and Isabella both, but he wanted time alone with Dana. He'd had enough of the double-dating scene.

Isabella nudged Danny discreetly with her elbow, and Tom appreciated the gesture. "Maybe we'll see you later at the auditorium," Isabella put in smoothly. "Danny and I are stopping for coffee first. I need my caffeine fix for the night."

Danny looked mildly surprised before recognition dawned on his face. "Oh yeah, right," he said. "I guess we should be going. Talk to you guys later."

Tom waved as Isabella dragged Danny into

the night. *That's a relief,* he thought. Of course Isabella was a direct conduit to Jessica, which meant that Elizabeth would find out he was on a date with someone else—someone beautiful and charming. He shrugged to himself. *So what if she does? I don't care. In fact, I hope she finds out.*

Dana gently brushed her fingertips against Tom's back. "Your friends are nice. They're really popular too. I remember noticing them right away when I started at SVU." She smoothed back her glossy hair with her free hand. "I'm not surprised that you hang out with Sweet Valley's best."

Tom laughed and pulled her closer. "I'll have to tell them that. They'll be flattered." They were just outside the auditorium where the reading was being held. People swarmed around the entrance. Even though it wasn't Maya Angelou herself reading tonight, her work was popular enough to draw a crowd.

Tom and Dana made their way through the packed auditorium and found two seats fairly close to the stage. Tom settled comfortably in his chair and glanced around the auditorium. In the sea of faces he'd recognized more than a few people, some from classes and some from WSVU. Tom pretended not to see them; he didn't want any reminders of his past. *Tonight is the night I get*

201

on with my life, Tom vowed silently. *Tonight is all about the future—and Dana.*

"This is perfect," Dana murmured to Tom. "This whole night's been perfect."

Tom dropped an arm around Dana's shoulders and stroked her hair as she snuggled closer. "You're absolutely right, Dana." His eyes met hers for a long second. "Let's hope this is only the beginning."

Chapter Thirteen

"Hey, Nina, I'm over here," Elizabeth called, jumping up and down and waving her poetry program high in the air. Nina finally caught Elizabeth's eye and waved before she began squeezing her way through the crowd.

"Whew! I'm glad I found you, Liz," Nina gasped. "I got a little worried when I saw how packed the place was. I didn't think this many people liked poetry."

"Maybe not poetry, exactly. I bet it's more that they like Maya Angelou." Elizabeth handed Nina the extra program she'd taken for her.

Nina skimmed through it. "Wow! They're going to have different poets reading selections of Maya Angelou's work. Then they'll be reading their own original work inspired by her. This should be something else."

Elizabeth gave her a little hug. "I'm so glad you agreed to come with me, Nina. You look great," she remarked, noting Nina's tailored, yellow linen suit and cream-colored silk blouse.

"Thanks," Nina replied. "Actually I feel a little overdressed."

Elizabeth watched the students hurrying into the auditorium. *Nina's not out of place here at all. Everyone looks so sophisticated here tonight,* Elizabeth thought a little wistfully. Elizabeth was still in her gray tunic and tights; she had only had time to throw her backpack and cap into a student union locker and then race over to meet Nina.

Oh, well, she concluded, *Nina doesn't mind how I'm dressed. That's the best part about going out with your girlfriends. You don't have to be self-conscious about how you look.*

"Thanks again for the invite, Liz," Nina said. "I wouldn't have even known about this reading if it weren't for you."

"Hey, it's my pleasure. You know, this night got off to a pretty boring start, but I think it's turning out to be great," Elizabeth bubbled.

"You can say that again. Liz, you don't know how grateful I am that you rescued me from another night entombed in my room."

Elizabeth chuckled at Nina's dramatic words.

"Don't even laugh. I couldn't face another weekend of sheer studying!" Nina added.

"You work too hard," Elizabeth declared. "We *both* do, which is why we deserve our girls' night out!"

Nina grinned. "No boys allowed," she cracked.

The people who had been handing out programs suddenly put them aside and disappeared into the auditorium. Only a few people remained lingering at the entrance to the auditorium.

Nina pointed toward the entrance. "Hey, we'd better go in, or we'll never find a seat."

"I hope we're not stuck sitting way in back." Elizabeth groaned as they hurried inside. "If we do, it'll be my fault for stalling."

The auditorium was nearly full. There was a steady buzz of voices as people settled in and got ready for the reading. Elizabeth couldn't spot a single empty seat, let alone two, for as far as she could see. Nina was right; it was amazing so many people had showed up.

Nina grabbed her by the hand and hurried toward the main aisle, her steps clicking noisily on the polished floor. "Look, there are two great seats down below. We won't have to sit in the nosebleed section after all. Let's grab 'em before someone else does."

Nina rushed on ahead, and Elizabeth followed her. Nina found her row and squeezed her way through the packed seats with remarkable dexterity. She finally plunked down, set her purse on the empty seat next to her, and frantically motioned for Elizabeth.

Nina's right. These are *excellent seats,* Elizabeth thought as she began worming her way through the row. *We're close enough to get a terrific view of the poets.*

Suddenly Elizabeth gasped and put her hand to her throat. Her heart seemed to plummet to her feet as she came to a dead stop. *I must be seeing things,* she thought, staring hard at the couple two rows ahead. *No, I'm not. It really is Tom—with another woman.*

Elizabeth desperately fought the urge to flee. *Why did Tom have to show up here of all places? He's all over that girl too! It's disgusting.* Against her will Elizabeth strained for a better look. The brunette turned to simper up at Tom, and Elizabeth could see she was very pretty. She clenched her teeth.

Elizabeth felt a tap on her arm, causing her to spin around. "Excuse me," said a man sitting right behind her, "but would you take your seat, please? You make a better door than window."

Farther down the row Nina was frowning

and waving for Elizabeth to come over. But the room was spinning too quickly for her to keep going. Her face was on fire, yet her body felt as cold as ice. Her stomach twisted and turned.

Finally, as if she were a robot, Elizabeth roughly shoved her way over to Nina. "I've got to go."

Nina gaped at her. "Whaaat? Why?"

Elizabeth jerked her head in the direction of the offending couple, and Nina craned her neck to see. "Elizabeth, what on earth . . ." Nina's words trailed off as her eyes became focused and sharp. "Oh, Elizabeth, I'm sorry—"

"Well, I'm not," Elizabeth panted, pushing her ponytail back with an angry gesture. "But I can't stay, Nina. I'm sorry. But . . . I just . . . I just can't!" With that Elizabeth whirled around and clambered past the same people seated in their row.

"Wait, I'll come with you," Nina called in an anxious voice.

"Stay, Nina, I want you to," Elizabeth urged, pausing midflight. "You can tell me all about it later." Elizabeth herself wasn't sure what she meant by *it:* the reading or Tom and that . . . other woman.

"Hey, come on," growled the same guy Elizabeth had blocked before. "Do you mind, or are you personally trying to ruin my evening?"

Elizabeth moved on without saying a word or looking back. She raced toward the exit just as someone tapped on the microphone, sending feedback through the auditorium like an electric charge. "Good evening, ladies and gentlemen, and welcome . . ." The booming words resonated through the walls as Elizabeth fled out the door.

The fresh, tart air was like a slap in Elizabeth's face, jarring her from her near hysteria. The dark night was a soft blanket covering the campus; Elizabeth wished she could hide under it, sheltering herself from humiliation and pain.

She began to run harder, her feet skimming the grass. Her throat was choked with sorrow. She sobbed uncontrollably as she pounded across the quad. People turned to stare, but she scarcely noticed them.

Suddenly Elizabeth tripped and fell, her foot catching on a rock. She crashed to the ground and lay for a split second, her knees burning and her hands aching. Pain radiated through her body. Gasping, she clambered awkwardly to her feet and stumbled forward, every cell in her body crying out for comfort.

Her pace slowed by the fall, Elizabeth took several deep breaths and dashed away the wetness from her eyes. *You needed that reality check, Elizabeth Wakefield,* she lectured herself over a pounding heart. *No matter how much it hurt.*

Her feet quickened as she scolded herself further. Her knee gave a sharp twinge with every footfall, but the pain raging inside her was far worse. *It's time you stopped burying your head in the sand. You were feeling sorry for Tom Watts, imagining that he was missing you. But it's obvious now that he doesn't miss you. In fact, he doesn't need you at all. He's recovered completely!*

Elizabeth sped across the quad as if pushed by some unknown force. She ached for warmth, understanding, and a gentle, familiar touch. And she knew she wasn't running aimlessly—not anymore. *Tom has made a new beginning in his life,* she told herself. *And it's time for you, Elizabeth Wakefield, to do the same!*

I need someone to hold me, Elizabeth thought. *I need Todd.* As Todd's dorm came into view she pushed harder. The world was a cold and lonely place right now. Only Todd could make things right.

This is the moment I've been dreading, Jessica moaned to herself. The night was clear and shining, the stars like diamonds in the velvety black sky . . . and Jessica was ready to crawl into the nearest hole. *Unfortunately there are no holes available. Or quicksand, for that matter. No place where I could conveniently disappear.*

Nick was banging on the shiny green door to the Foxes' colonial house. Meanwhile Jessica's knees were knocking and her stomach was on fire. She tried to slow her rapid breathing, but her galloping heart wouldn't allow it.

Nick shot her a get-your-act-together look before pounding again. He had spoken barely a word to her after their huge blowup in the car, and he no longer seemed to be in a comforting mood. *That's the way it goes,* Jessica thought. *Once his mother gets a good look at me, it'll all be over for us anyway. Still, I would have liked our last few minutes together to be nice ones.*

"I'm coming!" came a clear, commanding voice.

Jessica grimaced but mustered a weak smile for Nick's benefit. But when the green door opened, Jessica felt all her false happiness slip away. There she was, in the flesh—that dreadful woman who'd been making Jessica's last few days a living hell. It was Mrs. Fox! Jessica gulped loudly and prepared herself for the worst.

"Nick, why are you and your friend just standing there? Come on in," Mrs. Fox ordered. She held the door and motioned them inside.

Jessica trailed Nick as closely as possible.

Maybe if she hid behind Nick and kept to dark corners, Nick's mother wouldn't get a good look at her.

They entered a dimly lit foyer. "Watch your step. Sorry it's so dark," Mrs. Fox apologized. "The light went out in the overhead lamp, and we haven't had a chance to change the bulb."

Jessica looked up at the burned-out light fixture and silently thanked it.

Mr. Fox strode across the living room, a big smile on his face. He was an attractive, distinguished-looking man. "So, at last we meet Miss Wakefield," he declared in a deep voice.

Nick's mother turned to gaze at Nick and Jessica, her eyebrows raised expressively. "Yes, *at last* we get to meet the disappearing girl-friend."

Nick groaned. "C'mon, Mom, you promised . . ."

"Now, Rhoda . . . ," Mr. Fox interjected at the same time.

Even though Mrs. Fox seemed to be looking right at Jessica, she wasn't saying anything. *Could it be true?* Jessica wondered. *Doesn't she recognize me at all? Maybe she's forgotten. Or maybe she's just saving up her tirade for later.* Jessica swallowed long and hard. The suspense was killing her.

Mrs. Fox sighed and put her hands on her hips. "I'm always being picked on around here.

I didn't mean anything *bad*. I was just stating the truth." She squinted dramatically and moved her head from side to side as if Nick were some sort of annoying obstacle.

Jessica shrank back, her heart hammering in her chest. *Omigosh, I can't stand this anymore,* Jessica thought frantically. *Can't we just get it over with?*

Mr. Fox led the way to the living room. Jessica, right at Nick's heels, murmured, "I want to apologize to you both for missing dinner twice. I'm very sorry for the inconvenience."

Mrs. Fox switched on the lamp near the sofa. "Don't worry about it," she said. "You were sick. It's not like you had any control over the situation. Headaches have a mind of their own."

Nick's mother waved her hand at the three of them. "Go ahead and sit down, everyone." Mrs. Fox sank into an overstuffed pale green chair and crossed her legs. She reached across and turned the knob on the lamp, increasing the level of brightness.

Nick started forward but halted to pick up a magazine that had fallen off the coffee table. Jessica was so close behind him, she didn't have time to stop herself from crashing right into him. Nick gave her a funny look over his shoulder, but no one else seemed to notice. *I've made it this far,* Jessica thought as she took her place next to Nick on the love seat. *I should just try to relax. Who knows? Maybe I'm home free.*

"I have a philosophy, Jessica. Don't sweat the small stuff . . ." Mrs. Fox's words trailed off as her jaw dropped open in virtual slow motion. Her eyes grew round and her face paled as she staggered to her feet.

Jessica shuddered guiltily as Mrs. Fox gaped and pointed a quivering finger. "Y-Y-You," she stuttered. "It's *you!*"

All eyes in the room turned and stared at Jessica. Her heart thundering wildly, Jessica imagined herself under a hot spotlight in an interrogation room. She rose too, facing Nick's mother with as much boldness and courage as she could summon.

"You're not Jessica—you're her—you're Margaret! What are you trying to pull?" demanded Nick's mother. Her green eyes virtually snapped with anger, and she quaked as though she was having a seizure.

"Margaret?" Nick repeated loudly. His dark brows knitted into a frown. "Jessica, what's going on?"

"What are you talking about, Rhoda?" Mr. Fox asked.

Mrs. Fox's voice grew shriller. "This is the woman who crashed into my Lexus. Her name isn't Jessica. I distinctly remember her telling me on the phone that her name was Margaret."

"Oh no," Nick gasped as he sank back in the love seat.

"Oh yes!" Mrs. Fox thrust her face close to Jessica's. "I don't know what kind of scam you're trying to pull here, young lady, but you better fess up right now!"

Nick suddenly jumped up and put his arm around Jessica's shoulders. "Look, Mom, I know Jessica. You must be mistaken. I don't know why you think she's this Margaret person."

Jessica was stunned. The last thing she expected from Nick at this awful moment was for him to stand by her. Nick's blind defense was more generous and kind than she deserved after all the lies she'd fed him. She turned to him, awestruck, and saw nothing but caring and compassion written on his gorgeous face. How could she have expected anything less from a guy like Nick? She couldn't stop the hot, guilty tears from coming to her eyes, causing Nick's face to cloud over with suspicion.

"Sounds like a misunderstanding to me," Mr. Fox put in.

"I'm not nuts!" Mrs. Fox spun around and

faced her husband. "I know what I heard."

Jessica squared her shoulders. She knew she had to put a stop to this three-ring circus. She put two fingers in her mouth and blew—*hard*. Her whistle pierced the room sharply, making everyone turn to stare at her in alarm.

Jessica took a deep breath and stepped back from Nick's comforting embrace. "Nick, I can't lie to you anymore. Your mom is right. I did have an accident with her on the freeway."

Nick's eyes narrowed. "Jess . . ."

His mother tossed her head. "You see, everyone doubted me—"

Mr. Fox clambered to his feet and put his hand on his wife's arm, cutting her short. "Let Jessica continue," he said soothingly.

Jessica met Mrs. Fox's eyes. "When I got to your house that night, I recognized the Lexus and the license plate and realized who you were. So I took off. I invented the headache as an excuse because I was afraid once you met me and realized who I was, you would hate me." She flipped her sleek blond hair over her shoulder and caught Nick's eye. "I was worried that Nick would be angry if he found out, so I canceled the second dinner too."

Nick grimaced and ran his hand through his thick brown hair. "Jess, why didn't you just tell me—"

"That's not all," Jessica interrupted. "I realized I never gave your mother my name, just my phone number. So I decided to pretend I was someone named Margaret. I wanted to apologize and smooth things over, but we kind of got off on the wrong track." Jessica sniffed sharply. "I really wanted to meet you, Mr. and Mrs. Fox. More than anything. I practically begged Nick to introduce us. I never expected anything like this would happen. Honest."

A silence fell over the room. Even though Nick was standing right beside her, Jessica felt miserable and alone. *Now that the truth is out, it's over. Finished. Nick will never forgive me for lying to him like that—and I'd totally understand.*

Mrs. Fox cleared her throat and began to speak slowly. "I admit I was worried when I received your card and teddy bear, Jessica. I thought you might be a phony, gushy girl—the kind of girl who would be all wrong for my Nicky."

Jessica wondered why Nick rolled his eyes and made an irritated growling noise in his throat just then. But he didn't speak, and Jessica was too afraid to ask.

"Plus I was surprised that a girl with the audacity to sneak her way into my son's undercover assignments could turn out to be so cutesy and sticky sweet. I was expecting more of a Mata Hari." A smile spread across Mrs. Fox's face. "I started worrying you might be a real fake . . . and a real flake."

What was going on? Why did Nick suddenly let out all his breath and let his shoulders drop down like that?

With a candid grin Mrs. Fox lowered herself back into her chair and jerked her head commandingly toward her husband. "Why are you still standing there, Ben? Nicky? Jessica? Why doesn't everyone sit down?"

Nick sank into the love seat as if someone had pulled the rug out from under him. Jessica remained standing until Nick tugged her down beside him.

Jessica couldn't speak for several seconds. Everyone else was just sitting and staring dazedly in front of them. Finally Jessica coughed and managed to ask, "So, you're, uh, not mad?" The question seemed incredibly feeble, but she was too stunned to come up with anything more complex.

"Mad? Oh no, Jessica. On the contrary, I'm pleased," Nick's mother retorted cheerfully. "Pleased and relieved. Anyone who has the nerve to stand up to me, concoct a crazy scheme like yours, and then come face me in person has the guts and style I admire. Nick doesn't need a fluffy, cutesy little girl. Nick needs a real woman with spunk and brains." She threw a warm, approving look at her son, who sat beside Jessica as stiff as a zombie.

"I'm sorry, though," Jessica said timidly, "for everything."

Mrs. Fox shook her head. "Stop right there, Jessica. No more apologies are necessary. Let's just put that silly accident and everything else behind us."

"Um, OK, Mrs. Fox," Jessica replied haltingly. "It's a deal."

Suddenly Mrs. Fox vaulted out of her chair and over to the love seat. She bent over and planted a kiss on Nick's cheek. "Good choice, Nicky. She's a keeper."

Dazed, Jessica rubbed her forehead. "But I still don't understand. I was sure everyone would be upset. I mean, *really* upset."

"Well, I'm not," Mrs. Fox assured her with a pat on the shoulder. "In fact, I'm happy everything's working out so well."

"I'm glad too," Jessica squeaked. She smiled weakly as her gaze went from Mrs. Fox to Mr. Fox, taking care to avoid meeting Nick's eyes. "Thanks for giving me a fresh start."

"Think nothing of it." Mrs. Fox gave her husband a significant wink. "Ben, we'd better get our coats upstairs, or we'll be late for our reservation."

After Nick's parents left, Jessica began to squirm. *Great. Nick's parents may have forgiven me, but Nick won't—I know it. I've gone too far this time.* Jessica turned to face Nick timidly. He sure didn't look pleased.

Nick cleared his throat. "My mother's not exactly subtle. She dragged my dad out of here to give us some time alone, which is *exactly* what we need." Nick stretched his legs out in front of him and exhaled deeply. "My mom— she's a real piece of work."

"What about me, Nick? Are you upset? Do you hate me?" Jessica asked anxiously, finally meeting his soulful green eyes. "I should have confessed to you earlier, but I didn't want to lose you," she whispered, her lower lip trembling.

He sighed as he studied her face. "Jessica, Jessica," he said softly. "Spunk and brains, huh?" He held out his arms and smiled. "C'mere, you spunky and brainy woman."

Jessica giggled and snuggled against him. "So you forgive me," she purred.

"Well, it looks like I'll have to," he confirmed with a quick kiss on top of her head.

"Why's that?" she answered, not really caring to know. She caressed the side of his face and pulled him down for more personal attention.

"You can't fight my mom. If she says you're the woman for me, then she must be right," he answered teasingly. "Besides, who else could drive me crazy like you do?"

"No one," Jessica murmured, pressing her lips more firmly against his.

"Liz? What are you doing here?" Todd's face was overcome with surprise as he opened the door to his room. "Are you okay?"

Elizabeth found herself shaking with the effort not to collapse. She had run nonstop to Todd's room, even choosing to take the stairs instead of waiting for the elevator. "I have to talk to you," she said. "Can I come in?"

Todd stepped aside. "Sure." He closed the door behind them. Todd was in blue basketball shorts and a white T-shirt that clung to his muscular chest and abs. The tight shirt made his shoulders seem broader than ever.

"I'm sorry if I'm interrupting you," Elizabeth said shakily.

Casually Todd pushed a basket of clean laundry out of the way and removed several books from his bed. "Nah. I was just doing some reading. Some stud I am, huh? Hitting the books on a Friday night?"

Elizabeth tried to smile in response, but her

eyes filled with tears instead. Todd's face fell immediately.

"Elizabeth, what's wrong?" He put his hands firmly on her shoulders.

"If you're fed up with me and just want to tell me to leave, I wouldn't blame you," Elizabeth choked out, longing to fling herself into Todd's arms and weep without shame. "I know I've been really unfair to you lately. I've been confused, thinking that I don't know what I really want anymore."

"It's OK, Liz, I understand," he said softly. "This is a rough time for you." His face was outwardly warm and sweet, not clouded with impatience as it had been when he'd left her at Silly Sam's Diner.

"Todd, let me explain—"

"You don't have to explain anything." Todd took a small step closer, running a hand over Elizabeth's hair.

Elizabeth breathed in Todd's scent. He smelled freshly of soap and aftershave—a familiar smell that made Elizabeth feel safe. She allowed herself to ease a little.

"I'm not upset with you, Liz. Really, I'm not."

Elizabeth shook her head and gazed up pleadingly into his eyes. "You may not be upset now, but I know I've hurt you. And I'm sorry."

"Is that why you've come over tonight? To apologize?"

"Not exactly." Elizabeth wiped her eyes hastily and sniffed. "I—I realized something tonight. Something really important."

"What's that, Liz?" Todd asked with gentle concern.

Elizabeth hoped she could speak through the lump in her throat. "Todd, after so many false starts and mixed signals . . . I know now that I need you. Oh, Todd, I need you so much. You're the only man I want in my life. If it's not too late . . ."

Todd's troubled expression was replaced with a look of sheer happiness. "Are you saying you want me back, Liz? Do you really mean it this time?" he demanded hoarsely, his fingers gripping her slender shoulders.

"That's exactly what I'm saying," she whispered. "If you'll have me."

Todd's face flushed as he swept Elizabeth into his arms and hugged her tightly. "Do you have to ask?" he murmured into her neck as he stroked her hair with one hand, her back with the other.

Elizabeth gave in to Todd's embrace completely. She felt a charge up her spine as Todd's fingers gently grazed the nape of her neck. She turned her face up toward his expectantly. "Kiss me, Todd," she whispered urgently. "Kiss me."

Todd lowered his lips to hers and kissed her hungrily, pulling back to look deeply into Elizabeth's eyes. "It's you and me, then?"

"Yes, Todd." Elizabeth reached up to brush her lips softly against his. "It's you and me . . . forever."

"It's a bee-*yoo*-tee-ful morning in Sweet Valley. The skies are blue, and the sun is shining. Another perfect day in *gor*-geous Southern California." The pilot's voice flowed smoothly over the PA system. "Passengers will remain seated until notified otherwise. We will be disembarking in exactly eleven minutes. We're four minutes ahead of schedule, folks, so enjoy!"

Enjoy. Right, Gin-Yung thought dully. The plane had landed almost fifteen minutes ago, and it seemed unreal to her that she'd finally reached her destination. Gin-Yung unsnapped her seat belt as the light flashed off. A baby in the front of the plane began to cry.

Gin-Yung leaned back against the vinyl headrest and closed her eyes wearily. She knew exactly how that poor little kid felt. A lump swelled in her throat as she wished she could be that child, if only for a few precious moments. It would be heavenly to cry shamelessly, with abandon. A thin smile crossed Gin-Yung's face as she imagined what would happen if she went ahead and did it anyway.

Gin-Yung straightened her blazer and smoothed down her cotton shirt. *My skirt may be a little wrinkled, but luckily I still look OK,* she thought. *On the outside anyway.* She watched as some passengers restlessly got to their feet in spite of the attendants' warnings to stay in their seats. Gin-Yung herself was in no big hurry to get off the plane. For a minute she considered staying on and going wherever the plane went next. *Maybe I would get to see the whole world in just a matter of days.*

The flight to Sweet Valley had been over thirteen hours long, not counting layovers. But up in the air Gin-Yung felt safe. The airplane had been a sanctuary, a place of limbo where she could shut out grim reality. As long as Gin-Yung was floating in the sky she could pretend everything was fine and normal.

With a sigh Gin-Yung stared down at the silver charm bracelet on her right wrist. A miniature Tower of London dangled from the chain. It was kitschy and touristy to be sure, but Gin-Yung's heart had swelled when Jamie Lynn gave it to her.

I can't believe I've left London behind, Gin-Yung thought sadly. She and Jamie Lynn had cried in each other's arms when Gin-Yung told her that a family crisis had arisen, forcing her to give up her internship. That charm bracelet was a token of all the amazing things Gin-Yung was able to experience in London: Piccadilly Circus, Harrods, the Savoy Hotel, Westminster Abbey . . . the little shops, the pastries, the multiethnic cuisine . . .

Gin-Yung brushed a tear from her eye and twisted the bracelet around on her wrist. *I'll probably never see London again,* she thought, dark depression setting in. *Probably never see Jamie Lynn again.* And on top of it all she had missed the Spirit of Massachusetts–Whippets game. Someone else would get to write about the soccer match of the century.

While Gin-Yung was in London, her whole life had been turned completely upside down. Nothing would ever be the same. *I didn't want to come home like this, but I had no choice,* Gin-Yung thought anxiously. *Now I'm back in Sweet Valley, supposedly ready to face the most difficult challenge of my life.*

Gin-Yung craned her neck and tried to look out the small, smeary window. She couldn't see much. Someone riding a luggage cart. Another vehicle pulling up to refuel the plane. The airport itself was just a boring, boxy shape. Gin-Yung could imagine her family anxiously waiting inside the terminal. She gripped the armrest apprehensively. *I don't think I can handle them all today. They'll be too emotional and excited. . . .*

Gin-Yung's stomach lurched, and her mouth went dry. She licked her bloodless lips and struggled to keep her composure as static crackled over the loudspeakers. "I hope you enjoyed your flight with Sweet Valley International. Passengers may now leave the aircraft. Thank you for choosing to fly with Sweet Valley International today."

Gin-Yung stood and reached under her seat for her tote bag. She took measured, calming breaths as she waited for the passengers ahead of her to file out. *Well, here goes,* she thought. *It's time.*

Minutes later Gin-Yung was making her way slowly toward the terminal. Suddenly a wild blur of noise and motion enveloped her as she entered the airport. An excited swarm of people brushed past her. It was hot and stuffy; Gin-Yung had to struggle in order to breathe properly.

"Gin-Yung!" shrieked a voice. "Gin-Yung!" cried two more familiar voices. Gin-Yung reluctantly turned around.

The Suh family descended upon her. Gin-Yung's mother led the pack, her small, plump form charging with outstretched arms. A small part of Gin-Yung ached to run back to the plane, back to her sanctuary. She wasn't ready to face her family . . . not yet.

"My baby," Mrs. Suh sobbed. She flung her arms around Gin-Yung, who felt herself stiffening. "Oh, I've been so worried."

Mr. Suh reached his broad arms around and hugged both wife and daughter. His thin face was pale, and his dark-rimmed glasses somehow looked too big on his face. Gin-Yung could tell that both her father and mother hadn't been sleeping well. Her heart sank even further when she noticed how much her parents had aged over the short period she'd been in London. Worry and stress had etched new lines in their faces and put more gray in their hair.

Guilt, pain, and exhaustion were all battling for Gin-Yung's attention. *Don't they understand that I want to be treated normally?* she cried out silently. *I don't want people hovering over me. I just want to be alone right now.*

"Are you hungry, Gin-Yung? Or thirsty?" Her father's voice was thick and strained. "Can we get you anything?"

Before Gin-Yung could reply, her two sisters surged into the melee after waiting patiently behind their parents. The oldest of the family, Kim-Mi, was struggling to be composed, but she soon gave in to tears. "Gin-Yung," she sobbed. "You look so thin. We should take you to the restaurant right away."

"I'm fine," Gin-Yung said quickly in a low voice. "And I'm not hungry." *I just want to leave this place,* she thought angrily. *Can't you see that?*

Chung-Hee was only seven and had no qualms about showing her emotions. She hadn't stopped screaming Gin-Yung's name. Now she clung to Gin-Yung's arm, her face wet and red. "I didn't get to hug Gin-Yung yet," she whined, trying to work her way into the tight huddle.

In the center of the mess Gin-Yung froze. She stared straight ahead, her lips set in a tight, determined line. "Please stop crying. Let's be positive, OK? There's no reason to fall apart."

As her family began backing away reluctantly, Gin-Yung looked around the crowded terminal. "Where's Byung-Wah?"

"Your brother is here," Mrs. Suh said in a soft, quavering voice. "Your grandmother is here too. She was thirsty, so Byung-Wah went with her to get a glass of water. He's very helpful, Gin-Yung. He's sixteen now . . . almost grown up."

Gin-Yung nodded distractedly. *It's up to me to show them that everything will be OK,* she realized. Determination flowed through her. *I'll have to be the strong one; I can see that already. But I can handle it. . . .*

"Why don't I go ahead, then," Gin-Yung said in her briskest voice. "You guys can meet me later." But as Gin-Yung took one step forward, the room began to spin in a dizzying circle. Blindly she reached for her mother's arm. Silver spots suddenly appeared before Gin-Yung's eyes. Her family's faces blurred as everything around her began to go dark. Gin-Yung sank to the floor, her consciousness slipping away as Mrs. Suh leaped forward to catch Gin-Yung before her head hit the ground.

Elizabeth and Todd are finally back together. But will Gin-Yung's unexpected return tear them apart? Find out in Sweet Valley University #28, **ELIZABETH'S HEARTBREAK.**

Created by Francine Pascal

Ask your bookseller for any titles you may have missed. The Sweet Valley University series is published by Bantam Books.

SWEET VALLEY HIGH™

Created by Francine Pascal

The top-selling teenage series starring identical twins Jessica and Elizabeth Wakefield and all their friends at Sweet Valley High. One new title every month!

SWEET VALLEY HIGH™

All Transworld titles are available by post from:
Bookservice by Post, PO Box 29,
Douglas, Isle of Man IM99 1BQ

Credit Cards accepted.
Please telephone 01624 675137 or fax 01624 670923
or Internet http://www.bookpost.co.uk
or e-mail: bookshop@enterprise.net for details.

Free postage and packing in the UK.
Overseas customers allow £1 per book (paperbacks)
and £3 per book (hardbacks)